Iris Brown Lit Mag, founded in 2013,
is a literary magazine exploring the histories, cultures,
experiences, and sensibilities of women who identify as LGBTQIA.

978-0-9857056-4-0

Iris Lit Mag Brown

Publisher's Note

Welcome to the inaugural issue of *Iris Brown Lit Mag*! The origins of this publication begins with a personal story—my story, so let's take a trip back to 2012.

During that summer, as I sat in awe of the boldness that characterized an eighteen-year-old lesbian poet who stood on a stage before a large crowd, fanning the flames of her soul for all to see, I saw myself. I saw who I might have been if I had not settled into a neatly packaged, socially acceptable, heterosexual lifestyle. I saw who I might have been if I had grown up admiring proud, same-sex-loving idols like Doria Roberts, Ellen DeGeneres, or Wanda Sykes, or if I had LGBTQIA elders to confide in, or gay-friendly books to read. Most importantly, I saw who I needed to be from that day forward. Me. I needed to be *all* me *all* the time—devoid of shame, guilt, or apology. No more hiding, no more repressing the undeniable truth that I had known since I was in fourth grade. No more trying to fit into the straight woman mold. I needed, more than anything in the world, to be whole, and to be open to experiencing whole love—natural love, the kind of love that is free from social additives, preservatives, and other artificial perspectives.

What I did not anticipate was that my decision to free myself in this way would ultimately affect my writing. Suddenly, the lesbian characters that I had imprisoned in a steel vault in the pit of my closeted hell, broke free along with me, and came rushing onto the page, infusing in my writing a level of emotional integrity that I had never before known. Right away, my short story, "Lib," was accepted for publication in *Weave Magazine*. This piece explores the world of a lesbian mom who, along with her wife, and in the midst of attempting to be whole for her daughter, attempts to rebuild her life after having been raped in her own home. It was in my quest to publish this story and others that I discovered how sparse my LGBTQIA-friendly options were. So I decided to create a safe literary space for other writers, a space that is perpetually eager to publish literature and art that explores the histories, cultures, experiences, and sensibilities of women who identify as LGBTQIA.

Not only is Iris Brown now on the map, she is a sister publication to *94 Creations*, a mainstream literary journal on its fifth issue. Both titles are projects of Literary League of Louisville, a newly established nonprofit. Our board members include Charlene Luck, Laura Caitlin Davis, Julia Crittendon, Erin Brady Pike, Amy Jackson, Libby Filiatreau, and yours truly.

Iris Brown Lit Mag's editorial team includes a fun-loving group of lesbians *and* straight allies, all of whom I love and am deeply grateful to know, and all of whom are committed to discovering fiction, creative nonfiction, and poetry that are diverse and sophisticated, and that range from the very subtle to the gritty and evocative. Their bios appear on the following page.

Additionally, we had the great pleasure of working with guest editors Stephanie Schroeder (creative nonfiction) and Pamela Sneed (poetry) to make final decisions about which works to publish. Their bios and interviews appear herein, and the value of their kind support will forever remain in our hearts.

As we continue to venture through this very important literary and socially necessary work we are doing, we hope we can count on your support, as well. Please:

- Let your writer and reader friends know about us,
- Like us on Facebook,
- Visit our website (www.irisbrownlitmag.com) and join our mailing list,
- Subscribe to *Iris Brown Lit Mag* and/or make a donation.

Thank you for your attention.

Sincerely,

Adriena Dame
Founding Editor

Editorial Team

Adriena Dame, author of *The Moo: Stories and a Novella* and publisher of *94 Creations* literary journal, is a professor of undergraduate creative writing courses at Spalding University, and a board member for Louisville Literary Arts, Kentucky Foundation for Women, and Generation iSpeak. She is co-chair of InKY Reading Series, Co-Founder/Designer of the SOSAJI! sock brand, designer of Damejoyas jewelry art, and she teaches English as a Second Language to immigrants and refugees in Louisville, Kentucky.

Charlene Luck is a fiction writer from the Greater Detroit Area. She is a graduate of the University of Michigan's MFA in prose program, where she completed her thesis, a collection of short stories titled "In Your Houses." Her short story, "Grey Herons," was a finalist in the Glimmer Train Stories Summer Short-Short Fiction Contest 2007. She lives in Louisville, Kentucky with her husband, Jeff, and three cats: Manny, Mike, and Cheszwyck.

Julia Crittendon is the publisher of *Metamorphosis: Inspirational Stories of Women Living with Alopecia* (her success story is featured in the December/January 2012 issue of *Ebony Magazine*). A woman of many hats, she is co-founder of SOSAJI!, an emerging, private-label sock company; she is the mind and muscle behind Jai's Fitness; and she is the director of Generation iSpeak, a youth-centered non-profit organization designed to facilitate learning and exploration in the areas of literacy, arts, and education.

Laura Caitlin Davis is a student in Spalding University's low-residency MFA in Writing Program, and holds a BA in Anthropology from the University of Louisville. She has worked as an editor for several years. Her stories appear in The Heartland Review and The One Million Stories Project. On her wrist, she sports a black and purple tattoo she calls her "perpetual purple prompt." It reads Ecrivez, a French word that essentially means, "Dude, you better write!"

Deena Lilygren holds an MA in English Literature from the University of Louisville, and now attempts to spread her love for literature around her new stomping grounds at Elizabethtown Community and Technical College. As the main complaint of her undergraduate creative writing classmates was that her characters were all lesbians, she is unsurprised and quite pleased to find herself working with *Iris Brown Lit Mag*.

Contents

Otha "Vakseen" Davis III

Otha "Vakseen" Davis III regards music as the driving force behind his business career, and his passion for the arts has been key to maintaining his sanity in the fast-paced entertainment industry. Drawing inspiration from women, relationships, emotions, music, and the African American experience, his mixed medium paintings have been sold to collectors and art enthusiasts throughout Los Angeles and the Southeast region of the United States. While he has only been on the art scene at a professional level since January 2012, Otha has been selected for solo and group exhibitions in Los Angeles' Noho Art Gallery, Santa Clarita City Hall, Norbertellen Gallery, Dysonna City Art Gallery, Stay Gallery, Larrabee Sound Studios, Aquarium of the Pacific, The Met Gallery 950, Media Temple Studios, Bob's Espresso Bar, M. Bird Salon and Atlanta's Emerging Art Scene Gallery, amongst others. His work has has also been selected and featured in over twenty-five art and literary magazines.

Process

"Heartache Sit Down" is a part of my Jazz^3 collection. In this series, I pay tribute to the greats through vibrant, emotional, cubism-based art. Music has always played a major role in my life. I grew up listening to Jazz and a number of other genres, from Dizzy and Coltrane to Miles and Billie Holiday. Using a fine mixture of warm and cool acrylic tones, I was able to play off the portrait's natural energy and provide balance and allure. This is actually one of my favorite pieces in the collection.

Heartache Sit Down

13 . Otha "Vakseen" Davis III

Stephanie Schroeder

Stephanie Schroeder, author of *Beautiful Wreck: Sex, Lies & Suicide*, a memoir, is a lesbian-feminist writer and activist living in Brooklyn, New York. Her work has been published in *That's Revolting: Queer Strategies for Resisting Assimilation*, *Hot & Bothered: Short Short Fiction on Lesbian Desire*, and others.

Interview

I.B. Why do you write?

S.S. I love writing! I like to tell stories, whether they are mine or other folks'. It's important that our stories be told, especially women and especially lesbians, but really all people who have been, and still are, erased from history, or who's history someone else writes about/for them. I won't let that happen to my sisters or me while I'm on writing watch.

I.B. Describe how you discovered your voice as a writer?

S.S. I'm a pretty workmanlike (workwomanlike?) writer. I'm a trained journalist, so my writing is very reportorial in style. I went from being a shy teenager who was studying fashion design at a vocational school to studying communications at a university. I didn't know then that my choice was really so I could face the world and tell my own stories—stories that were already happening and yet to happen. Writing was and is a way for me to express myself. I'm certainly no orator, but writing comes naturally. I'm so much better on paper! I'm a documentarian and I write sparely and economically. I'm not very wordy. I don't like flowery descriptions or overblown language. Honest and raw is how many characterize much of my work. I just think it's real.

I.B. Tell about a time when you felt like your work as an activist incited positive and evident social change.

S.S. It's hard to say, in the larger scheme of things, what directly incites change and what does not. I think it's the power of many people, usually not one person (although sometimes this is the case) which incites change.

I spoke with a group of drama therapy students in the spring. They were all eager to hear a mental health consumer's point of view. I read a very brief passage from my book and referred to a social worker who, in my story, I just rolled my eyes at and thought was useless in my recovery. One young woman asked me how she (and the whole group) could work with clients to not be that social worker who consumers roll their eyes about and disregard. Then we all had a discussion about what it looks like for mental health professionals to be truly helpful. That was a very powerful moment for all of us.

I.B. What is one of the most challenging obstacles you've had to face in your writing life? How did you overcome it?

S.S. Well, of course, trying to make a living as a writer is nearly impossible. The few who do are quite fortunate. Then, there is trying to get published. Publishing a book is far different than publishing an article in a magazine, newspaper, or online outlet.

When I started shopping *Beautiful Wreck*, I had one agent, out of more than two dozen I contacted, who was interested. She loved the book, but said she was only ninety-nine percent sure she could sell it and it was that one percent against me that made her pass on it after a lot of back and forth. Many agents and publishers said it was too brutal, others didn't even believe all of the stuff in the book happened to me. Another agent I met late in the game, Charlotte Sheedy, also loved the book. However, she said she was too old and already had too much on her plate. She manages a lot of big deal lesbian and feminist writers like Sapphire and Eve Ensler and also the estates of some iconic lesbian and feminist writers such as Audre Lorde. That was very encouraging to me at the time. But no one else in mainstream publishing was ever again interested in my book. I had to do a workaround and find a publisher who would publish me, which I finally did. But, the whole process soured me on the mainstream publishing industry, such as it is. Just as similar journeys to publication have soured other writers. Indie presses are the future of publishing.

I.B. If you were a sentence, what would you say?

S.S. Please do not follow any script that is not written by and for you.

I.B. It is common for people's definitions of success to revolve around financial and social status. Are these the terms you use to define success? If not, how do you define success?

S.S. This is common in the world-at-large, but not in the queer and feminist and artistic communities in which I live here in New York City. So, it's not really an issue for me. I am not at all materialistic, I own very little, and I have moved and given away every material possession I've had many times over. I deplore the idea of social or financial status being a measure of success. How very one percent!

Of course, we all need dough to survive, but beyond a modicum of money to cover necessities... I define success as doing what one wants and needs to do and doing it in the most effective manner and in the least harmful way possible. I think most people are creative whether they utilize outlets for creativity or not. I find it very sad that people "give up" writing or music or sports or whatever for other people. Living according to one's own rules—and dreams, is not selfish; it's sane and healthy.

I.B. What/who do you like to read?

S.S. I only read nonfiction. I've been through a lot, a whole lot, and I cannot suspend my disbelief for any amount of time to read a novel or any sort of fiction. I especially like to read memoirs and biographies, political essays/tracts (surprise!), and sometimes poetry. While I appreciate a great deal all that goes into creating a work of fiction, I am not interested in the genre at all.

I.B. What words of wisdom do you have for women who write?

S.S. To actually do it: write. Don't just talk about writing or say you're a writer: WRITE! And don't let anyone shut you up or shut you down. Don't sacrifice or stop writing for anyone or anything. And no one who truly cares about you would ask that of you. We must remember Tillie Olsen's "I Stand Here Ironing" as a great work of literature generally, but also a great work of women's literature and of women writers' herstory. Her work is also cautionary.

Marcie Bianco

Marcie Bianco, Queer Public(s) Intellectual, PhD, is a columnist and contributing writer at *AfterEllen* and *Lambda Literary*, as well as an adjunct associate professor at John Jay College at Hunter College. Her current projects include a scholarly manuscript about the anti-humanist, materialist ethics of English Renaissance Drama, and a memoir about lesbian academic affairs. She lives in Brooklyn with her pup, Deleuze.

Interview

I.B. Why do you write?

M.B. The reason I write is threefold: writing nourishes my creative spirit; it engages the cerebral-side of me and allows me to work on myself; and, because writing for me is both an ethical and aesthetic endeavor, it is how I feel I can contribute to the feminist, lesbian, and queer communities in terms of creating and engaging in cross-cultural dialogues.

I.B. If you were a book, what book would you be? Why?

M.B. While I think in terms of emotion—of verve and passion, of power and the erotic, I am more of Nietzsche's *The Gay Science* or Audre Lorde's *Zami*, and I think I would actually be *Montaigne Les Essais*, a variegated collection of philosophical essays, entrenched in skepticism and materialism, serious yet subtly satirical.

I.B. Do you consider yourself a feminist? If so, how do YOU define feminism?

M.B. More than anything else, I identify as a feminist. In simple terms, feminism is a political ideology with a two-pronged objective: the eradication of (white, patriarchal) oppression and the championing of difference. The latter is imperative and occurs most profoundly in the realms of ontology and ethics. The championing of difference entails the rethinking of our bodies, our actions, and how we come to knowledge. In terms of epistemology alone, for example, we have historically privileged sight over the other senses in knowledge production. This is where the work of feminists like Audre Lorde, Elizabeth Grosz, and Sara Ahmed hold critical significance. Unmoored from the latter objective, the former, of fighting systemic oppression, consequently manifests as idle rhetoric (most evident, these days, in the much-bandied accusation, "privilege!").

I.B. Share something interesting about yourself that has nothing to do with writing/ publishing.

M.B. I wanted to be President of the United States when I was younger. I know many kids have this fantasy, but I was actually very active in politics throughout my college years—I served as President of the Harvard College Democrats and President of the Massachusetts College Democrats; I interned in D.C.; and I worked on Al Gore's presidential campaign for nearly three years.

I.B. You have been given an opportunity to write the last sentence you will ever write. What is that sentence?

M.B. "Marcie said she would write the sentence herself."

Masochism and Academia: My Master, My Shakespeare

It has become increasingly evident to me that the quality of masochism I perceive as a vital component to my sexual relations has also functioned as equally vital to my sustained interest in academia.

The thread of masochism theoretically, if not yet ethically, became apparent as early as a Master's Shakespeare course, when I decided to recite one of Helena's monologues from A Midsummer Night's Dream for the required twenty-five-line recitation exercise. One of a handful of Shakespeare's female masochists, Helena—especially the Helena played by Calista Flockhart—was my kindred spirit. We were masochists for and in love; we would prostrate ourselves, shed ourselves of all dignity and self-respect, just for a morsel of affection.

Helena's words echoed in my head well past the class time allocated to the discussion of the play. My lines were set—the exchange, in 2.1, where Helena begs Demetrius to love her, even though he adamantly insists that he does not, nor cannot, love her:

> And even for that do I love you the more.
> I am your spaniel; and, Demetrius,
> The more you beat me, I will fawn on you:
> Use me but as your spaniel, spurn me, strike me,
> Neglect me, lose me; only give me leave,
> Unworthy as I am, to follow you.
> What worser place can I beg in your love …
> Than to be used as you use your dog?

This declaration is the mold of masochism I poured myself into during my education, before I read Freud, or Deleuze, or any of the queer scholars who articulated the concept for me in abstract terms. I had, and used, Helena's words to help me become the best possible spaniel to my Master…as well as to all the other women I encountered along the path to completing three graduate degrees. Ten years of "becoming masochist" fixed the identity—one that only exists in relation to our mutual dependence with another (the sadist)—into a permanent position. Regardless of whether my sadists were scholars, I actively sought out intimate relations with cold, cruel women to dominate me. The repetition provided comfort through familiarity; I knew my position. Furthermore, my willful submission to these women —suggestively, always older women, by at least ten years—fostered the libidinal sphere of fantasy that clouded over the reality of all these relations. The relation was born in reality but bred in fantasy.

And what better plane of immanence for this fantasy than Shakespeare?

***

My fantasy was green and ripe that summer after my graduation. The domain was virtual —the most apropos for fantasy to thrive, no?

The fastidiously layered structure of desire manifest in our virtual daily living—consistent electronic communication from 6:00 a.m. until 11:00 p.m. or midnight, primarily between Master and me, but also between her partner, Ellen, and me, and even the occasional email à trois—proved the ultimate stimulation to creating an unparalleled work ethic. They were both academic superstars—"academidykes"—in the humanities. I related to them in a variety of ways: I wanted to be both of them, I wanted to fuck both of them; I wanted to be their intellectual colleague and their culturally savvy mentee; and, most Oedipally, I wanted to be their child, the genetic offspring of their intellects.

I wanted to accompany them to conferences, dressed in all black, and hear the whispers of envious colleagues: "She is theirs."

Many scholars short-circuit at the thought of human contact. The only way they know how to commune in the flesh and have a discussion with eye contact is within the frame, or under the pretense, of the academic conference. This is especially true of literary scholars, cerebral creatures who regard the word as flesh and whose economy—and excellence—is language. Caricatured as isolated, depressed types, hunched over the glowing screen of the 21st century leather-bound book, the academic has actually become the everyman, who, in turn, has become nothing less than the avatar—for what has human kind become other than a collection of plugged-in bodies, alone in cubicles and bedrooms, with fingers that mindlessly flit on keyboards to conjure virtual selves in virtual domains?

***

That summer, my economy was Shakespeare. I consumed it; I exchanged and bartered (in) it. Master, Ellen, and I worked tirelessly on "the big Shakespeare book," which was to be marketed as the quintessential Shakespeare resource for both the scholarly and lay readers. While I conducted library research at Widener, wrote the annotated bibliography, and copyedited, Master and Ellen worked from Nantucket, writing and revising chapters. Master was like the queen bee, issuing out demands, while Ellen and I were the dedicated worker bees. Instead of buzzing in circular patterns, we communicated the nectar of our work through the electronic missive. As the summer progressed, Master and I refined our linguistic economy to an efficacious science of aphorisms and acronyms:

> To: Master
> From: Marcie Bianco
> Date: July 21, 2002
> Subject: no no no
>
> Okay, let me get this straight. You want to move AYLI before H5 and JC, just to have two comedies together? And yet you're moving MND behind RJ, which separates MND from LLL (another comedy) and places it between two tragedies (Okay, RII is classified as a history). No no no. Okay with the MND move, but not the others, and here's why:
>
> 1. H5 is sometimes said to be composed between 1598-9
> 2. Thomas Platter records seeing JC on 21 Sept. 1599
> 3. The SR records AYLI as 4 Aug. 1600
>
> Of course, date of composition and date of performance are different, but the above points do hold some relevance here. I mean, is there any particular reason why you want to make this move, other than to regroup the plays by genre and make things look pretty?

> To: Marcie Bianco
> From: Master
> Date: July 21, 2002
> Subject: Re: no no no
> Okay, this is why we pay you the big bucks. Ellen and I are persuaded. So we will move 1H6 and switch MND/Romeo.

To: Master
From: Marcie Bianco
Date: July 21, 2002
Subject: Re: no no no
Hooray! Point Bianco!
One more thing to confirm: Are we moving 2H4 ahead of MWW? Or leaving it between the H4s?

To: Marcie Bianco
From: Master
Date: July 21, 2002
Subject: Re: no no no
Ellen thinks/thought it was better to move the 2nd part so that MWW comes after them. Does this violate the Bianco rule of purity?

The alacrity with which we communicated, the speed of our correspondence, grounded and secured our trust in one another—or, more importantly, Master's trust in me—which demonstrated how well we worked together. An unparalleled concordia discors, my Master and me.

Naturally, then, our working relationship became more familiar, if not more intimate. Formality took a backseat to camaraderie—it was the summer, after all. Banter increased, particularly on my end, as I have the uncanny ability of transgressing almost every decorous boundary.

To: Marcie Bianco
From: Master
Date: July 26, 2002
Subject: website
While working on "Patrons of the Arts," I came upon Desmond Morris's website and found that in his bibliography he not only shows the book covers of all his books, but also gives links to where they can be purchased. Any way we can accomplish this feat?

To: Master
From: Marcie Bianco
Date: July 26, 2002
Subject: website
If you go to your website, you can click on the book images and each one will take you straight to Amazon. I already have it down, my Master!

To: Marcie Bianco
From: Master
Date: July 26, 2002
Subject: website
You're amazing. Thank you.

I delighted in calling her Master, and in acknowledging the identity she accepted it—I think she even took a sadistic pleasure in it. Yes, she is THE Master, MY Master. My idolatry, to my mind and to others, was the witty exposure of the primal ground of our working relationship. In calling attention to the S&M-like dynamic, I wasn't so much reifying the dynamic as I was satirizing it.

In recognizing one's subjected position, you take possession of it before others can possess it and take advantage of you.

***

Because of Ellen's terminal, degenerative illness, which progressively crippled her body, the crux of the email communication was between Master and me. Ours was the primary working relationship, even though Master and Ellen could technically talk with each other in person since they were residing in the same home. The absence of Ellen in our dialogue, however, affected a kind of triangulation that was sometimes sinister, sometimes awkward, and always over-determined.

Oftentimes I would wonder who the third person was in this relationship, me… or Ellen? My duty was invariably to my Master, but I knew to weigh Ellen's words carefully and not to automatically side with Master in all editorial disagreements. Ellen was Master's partner of twenty-five years, and that meant, especially in the later stages of Ellen's illness, that their partnership was primarily intellectual. They had co-written pieces in the past, and I knew, especially from this extant experience, that Ellen had an influential hand in all of Master's writing. Perhaps playing editor was part of her domestic duties.

Regardless, my intuition served me well, such that when Master would create a triangulated scenario—for example, via email—I knew the correct response was an interpretation of Ellen's famous rhetorical question, "Yes, no… and what else?" For example:

> Barbara says she cut the section on "Aeneas's Tale to Dido." That's not acceptable to me. I think readers need to know about the relevance of the Priam story, etc. Do you agree with me, or with her? I do think that PART of the graph on p. 508 can be cut, from "Hamlet; chooses….

Triangulation is all about compromise, right?

On the rare occasion, Master would counter-pose an editorial suggestion of mine against one of Ellen's and then remove herself from adjudication:

> *Ellen thinks your suggestion is fine. I'm willing to allow you two to decide.*

The parenthesis of our electronic discussions allowed for a certain suggestiveness that only Master could exquisitely spin:

> Ellen will look at it tomorrow, too. We may be able to add a little historicizing of the criticism that will point up this side of the story. (But, as I say, I think that kind of reading has now become so normative that it's not very interesting—and it also doesn't actually seem to me to be convincing. The play flirts—but it doesn't commit.)

Flirts indeed.

In all my life I never had, or have, met someone so indefatigable, someone with such an unflappable work ethic. Well, I've never met anyone beside myself who possessed that kind of dedication. Master was consumed by her work, perhaps out of habit, but also perhaps out of comfort and security, born out of a psychological need for avoidance.

Work was, ironically, a kind of respite from her personal life. Once, that August, she lamented to me her frustration at the loss of a proper holiday, to which I, in my slavish (and selfish) mentality, interpreted as an inadequacy on my part. Her response to my apology provided a rare glimpse at the woman underneath the black suit:

> *Don't be silly. I couldn't do any of this without you. I'm enormously grateful. My lack of holiday has as much to do with increased domestic responsibilities in the wake of Ellen's illness as it has to do with work. And work is what we like, right?*

Yes, we like work, my Master and me…. My Master, Myself.

***

It is postulated that the real power of the sadomasochistic relation is not held by the sadist but by the masochist. And I always did love power and had been attracted to its force. I think this argument holds true in the case of the caretaker, of the person who cares for another. The caretaker serves, and, therefore, can be construed as a kind of masochist, but in serving the caretaker controls; she controls the field of action and of engagement—she has discriminatory power. And it is in this latter sense that the caretaker is very much the sadist.

Master loved her caretakers—Ellen and me, as well as all the women who assisted her with her various administrative duties—because she saw us as secretaries, filters that determined what was and was not worthy of her attention. This was particularly true in terms of her professional career, where she was being pulled in a million directions by faculty from two different departments, by her students, and by her editors. I had become a gatekeeper, a protector of my Master, and I wasn't afraid to defend her when duty called. She, not surprisingly, was the target of numerous greedy poniards on campus.

Women really are our worst enemies; this is a symptom of patriarchy. There are only so many positions of power for women, so many slots available, so we all cut each other down in pursuit of those coveted posts. I really think men sit back and laugh at us as we attack each other. I think, too, that women attack each other in work settings when it will help align them with men in power—as if to say to those men, "I am one of you."

Master was the frequent target of catty and jealous women. Once, in an elevator in the Visual Arts Department, for which she served as chair, I slayed two women with my eyes when they criticized her for how she handled the department's administrative affairs. There was much hullaballoo around her tenure there. She was a literary scholar, not an artist, and the faculty in the department viewed her as the university's pawn who was strategically placed into the chair position in order to tame or help regulate the department. Master was the unwelcome interloper, and the faculty and staff—save one or two secretaries—went out of their way to combat her every move.

She even encountered opposition from her peers in the English Department. One female scholar in particular, who was dating the current university president, had a seething hatred of Master for no known reason other than jealousy. This Green-Eyed Bitch made a mistake, however, when she accidentally sent an email to my college roommate, where she was ranting about how she despised Master and didn't want her to become the next English Department chair. The email was intended for the extant department chair, but the idiot misspelled the email address and it landed into my roommate's inbox, which she promptly forwarded to me because she knew I was serving Master. At first I brought the email to the attention of Harriet, who had worked for Master for many years, because I wanted to shield

Master from Green-Eyed's negative energy. A few months later, on the eve of a stressful department meeting, I brought the email to Master's attention as a precautionary measure. She simply smiled at me with appreciation and said, "I've been in this department for over twenty years; I know who to trust…and I am aware of certain personalities."

From this unwavering loyalty and allegiance, in addition to my tireless work ethic, I earned my Master's love. Electronic missives of thanks were met with presents in the post, from chocolates and dried fruits on my birthday ("Eat the cranberries," she wrote on the card, "They're good for you"), to a handcrafted mahogany jewelry box at the end of a particularly arduous manuscript-proof cycle. The day before I left for my graduate studies at Oxford, the ladies of the Humanities Center threw me a going-away party, and my Master presented me with a gorgeous red leather wallet filled with British pound notes to use when I arrived in England.

Master gave me a hug and, holding me by both arms, smiled.

"Back to work?"

"Yes, back to work!"

We still had work to do. Even though I was scheduled to fly out of Logan the next day, I had to finish the index of another book project that Master was finishing up and fax it to the publisher before I left the States.

As my co-workers at the Humanities Center packed up their things and said their goodbyes, I took one more bite of the flourless chocolate cake they bought for my celebration and lingered in the hallway of the Center, the place that had become my home over the course of nine months. I hadn't felt like I had a home in years, and I had a growing unease in my stomach signifying my fear of departure from all the comforts of the familiar—the Humanities Center, my colleagues, and my Master.

I didn't want the night to end. I didn't want to leave my home.

I waved to Harriet as she gave me a wink and walked out the door.

Once again, I thought, home alone.

I turned, walked past Harriet's office and into Master's. At first I sat in the leather chair—the same leather chair in which I sat when I first interviewed for the job the previous October—and sighed. But, instead of the exhalation expressing that anxious energy and regaining a sense of calmness, my anxiety reinforced itself. I jumped up and walked over to the bookshelves that lined the walls of Master's office. Every single Arden edition of Shakespeare's plays were there; I re-shelved the handful of 3rd series Hamlets that had been carelessly interspersed among the other plays.

Running my fingers along the broken spines, I made a course around the perimeter of her office, then moved with trepidation to Master's desk. I sat down in her black leather swivel chair once again and lowered my fingers onto the keyboard—where her fingers have laid so many times—with intention.

I checked my email. Two missives from Master with reminders about the index. After replying in acknowledgement and with reassurance, I opened the index document and went to work, combing through the entire 300 page manuscript and documenting every mention of every noun, from "Arnold, Matthew," to "Shakespeare, William."

I was grateful for the radio silence from Master so I could finish my final task without interruption, even though I would never shirk contact from her. She must have finally gone to bed, I thought, as I read the computer clock: 1:03 a.m.

I stretched my arms above my head and decided to take a break. Grabbing my keycard, I walked out of the Humanities Center and towards the bathroom, peed, washed my face, and then decided to raid the Barker Center's food closet for whatever was left. Goldfish and seltzer water, what had become staples of my diet that summer, greeted me as the sole inhabitants of the closet. I took a bottle of seltzer, filled a plastic cup with artificial fish, and headed back to the Humanities Center.

1:29 a.m.

There was still two-thirds of the manuscript to work through before I left; not to mention the fact that I still had to pack my things and clean the room I was subletting near Central Square.

5:43 a.m.

The exhaustion that was creeping through my body for the past couple of hours had fully set in; I was tingling with tiredness. I breezed through the last pages of the manuscript and sent the draft of the index to Master for the final look-over. Then I gathered up my things and ran out of the Center, down Quincy and onto Cambridge Street, where I kept running, in the middle of the street, until I reached my apartment.

Nothing was packed, but clothes were strewn everywhere as if an attempt had been made, when in actuality it was just the current state of affairs. I bundled all my clothes into units—underwear, tees, pants—and stuffed them into my oversized, maroon Harvard duffle bag. Thankfully, I had already shipped my books, so I didn't have to worry about them, although I kept Ellen's copy of The Feminist Difference out of the shipment and placed it into my backpack, which I'd bring as a carry-on.

I started shaking from nerves, from sadness, and from exhaustion. I stripped down and hopped into the shower, which was ringed with dirt and brewed a dark-greenish mold in the corners. After a quick towel-off, I threw on a grey Boston tee and yoga pants, zipped up my sea-foam green Harvard hoodie, and hastily secured my black, Quicksilver backpack onto my shoulders, heaved my duffle bag over one shoulder, and set off, one last time, for the Humanities Center.

It was a little after seven when I arrived, and Master still had not responded to my queries about the index. So I unloaded the life I had been carrying on my back and decided to get a cup of coffee from the Starbucks down the street. Next door to Starbucks was an overpriced market from which I grabbed a bag of dried apple slices and a day-old, cold chicken burrito. Sucking, more than sipping, my caffé misto, I gingerly walked back to the Humanities Center. By the time I sat down at Master's desk, I had one message from her in my inbox:

Magnificent. Such a heroic undertaking. Ready to send.
Safe travels,
M

The swelling of my heart blushed onto my face. Heroic! My Master thinks I'm heroic! And I was. The email, more than the coffee, reinvigorated my body, and, without losing a breath, I faxed the two-dozen pages of the index to the publisher.

The fax beeped to let me know the pages were received. I let out a sigh, and in that moment my body deflated. The adrenaline rush was gone, and exhaustion returned once again. I slumped into one of the black leather chairs in Master's office and closed my eyes.

Brrrnnng-brrrnnng! Brrrnnng-brrrnnng!

My eyes shot open. It was 9:43 a.m. Brrrnnng-brrrnnng! I answered the phone.

"Good morning, the Humanities Center," I said by rote.

"Miss Maaarrrcie! It's Haaarrrrriet!"

"Hi, Harriet, dear!" I echoed back in delight.

"Miss Marcie, when are you off?" she said in her chipper Nebraskan voice.

"Oh, around noon, I think. Why?"

"Well, I won't be in today and I just wanted to say goodbye before you hopped on that big ol' plane to Englaaaand!"

"Oh Harriet, thank you! I'm going to miss you."

"I'm going to miss you too," she paused. "And you know Master is already missing you." I smiled.

"Yeah, I know."

I didn't add that I am going to miss her too, so, so much.

Missing Master didn't make logical sense—but emotions aren't logical. Our relationship was primarily virtual and, thanks to technology, we could continue our relationship regardless of either of our locations.

Around noon, I checked my email one last time. This was a time before iPhones and all the instantaneous pleasures of mobile devices, at least for my poor, student self, who still carried a flip-phone. I had to check my email now because I wouldn't be back online for at least 48 hours.

In my inbox sat one new email—from Master:

"Come back, little Sheba, anytime."

Tears. Hot tears on my flushed face. I didn't know the reference, but Master was always alluding to something, so I typed the sentence into Google. A Wiki entry was the first hit:

Come Back, Little Sheba (1952) is a drama film produced by Paramount Pictures which tells the story of a loveless marriage that is rocked when a young woman rents a room in the couple's house.... The title refers to the wife's little dog that was lost months before the story begins and which she still openly misses.

The synopsis goes on to explain that the young woman reminds the husband of how his wife
used to be in her younger days. As I scrolled through the Wiki page, my jaw slacked and then dropped entirely.

I was my Master's spaniel!

What worser place can I beg in your love,—
And yet a place of high respect with me,—
Than to be used as you use your dog?

This was the bone, and the boon, that I carried with me, along with my tears, out the door of the Humanities Center. At the corner of Quincy Street and Mass Avenue, I climbed into a cab that carried me away from my home to the airport.

To England. Oddly, to the home of Shakespeare, even though, to me, my home was with her.

Sarah Brooks, author of *The Beginning of Us*, a novella (Riptide Publishing, 2014), is a writer, a middle school English and history teacher, and a mother. She lives in Boulder, Colorado, where she is pursuing an MFA in Creative Writing at Naropa. Her work appears in *Sinister Wisdom, Room,* and other publications.

Interview

I.B. Why do you write?

S.B. Writing keeps me connected to the world and to myself—it has saved me, in many ways.

I.B. If you were a book, what book would you be? Why?

S.B. If I were a book, I'd be Louise Erdrich's *The Last Report of the Miracles at Little No Horse*. I keep secrets; I am not who I seem to be; everything around me in the world contains magic.

I.B. Do you consider yourself a feminist? If so, how do YOU define feminism?

S.B. I'm a feminist. I believe we continue to live in a world that limits women to a heterosexual marriage narrative, and that women empowering women (in friendships and/or in erotic relationships) can reveal new narratives and new strengths.

I.B. Share something interesting about yourself that has nothing to do with writing/publishing.

S.B. Something interesting about me: if I were not a parent, I would travel to Nepal and spend months in silence hiking and meditating at a monastery.

I.B. You have been given an opportunity to write the last sentence you will ever write. What is that sentence?

S.B. "I loved well."

The Story We Couldn't Find

Summer 2003. I enter a classroom on the first day of my graduate-level "Intro to Teaching" course, and A stands at the whiteboard, covering the surface with notes in black marker. I am 26; she is 34. She is my professor. Does something stir in me that first moment, besides a student's desire to impress? I don't think so. I am married to a good, kind man with whom I have traveled the world and come all the way to Alaska. What about A? When she turns around and sees me, does her heart beat faster at the sight of me, or does she merely regard me as a professor regards a student who appears bright-eyed, eager to learn? She is married, too, has two small children, has a whole life in this southeast Alaska town.

I study this picture of us, professor and student in the moment before language, and I wonder: If we had known what would happen in the next eight years, would we have still spoken the first words?

Our story begins. After a three-week class, she asks me to do my nine-month teaching internship in her high school classroom. We become friends: a weekend hike, an evening out for beers, dinner at her house with her family, hours planning lessons together. Each of our husbands jokes that finally his wife has found someone who matches her frenetic, restless desire to see the world. They're glad we've found each other.

One day in October at my apartment, A and I practice the scene between Olivia and Viola in Twelfth Night, so we can perform it for our ninth-graders. A disguised as a man, me beneath a veil, and suddenly we both feel—what? Laughing, we decide that's enough practice for one day.

Months later, at the end of the school year, A invites me to hike to a cabin with her. She tells me later that when she arrived to pick me up and found me in the sunshine staring out at the lake and the glacier, she felt overwhelmed by how beautiful I was. I tell her later I felt shy to skinny-dip with her in the lake by the cabin. But still, we are blind.

Summer 2004. Photographs. A and I on a mountaintop, A and I with her children on a beach. She leaves notes in my mailbox, Post-its on my door. I leave her silly gifts on her front porch. Late at night, we email each other long observations about our days, poetry. Our husbands shake their heads at our characteristic intensity.

I try to reconstruct the order of events. I examine our faces in the photographs, look for the placement of hands. When I re-read the poems, the notes, the long emails, I see why A's husband began to feel usurped. He was the first to raise the alarm. My husband believed me when I said I had never had a friendship like the one I had with A. I wasn't lying.

Fall 2004. A's husband asks us to stop communicating so much with each other; he wants her to focus on their marriage. I can't understand my despair. It's my first year with a real teaching job, but all I want is to share every thought with A, talk to her at every hour, be near her. She laughs so easily, her dark hair wild and beautiful around her face, I have never felt as content as I do playing with her children on the kitchen floor while she cooks curry at the stove. Her husband orders the cessation of email, no more weekly visits. And this is the hinge: what is forbidden becomes desirable.

We open secret email accounts; we send each other coded gifts through the school district mail; she pulls into my driveway with her kids in the car just to run into my apartment and hug me; we leave each other books with certain passages underlined. Maybe because we live in Alaska, or because we each grew up in conservative places, or because we have not read the right stories, neither of us understands what we are discovering. "Rare friends," we call ourselves. We rant to other friends about the craziness of her husband's behavior, the erection of the Berlin Wall that we work to scale. In our writing group, we produce essays about the rare friendship that can form between women, citing Emily Dickinson, Virginia Woolf, Eleanor Roosevelt. That is how little we know.

December 2004. A's husband travels somewhere to the East Coast for work, and my husband travels into the wilderness to do field work for the Forest Service. A invites me to dinner. We play with the kids, eat together, play some more, put the kids to bed. I wish I could share life with you like this, she says. In her son's room, I tell him a story, A leaning against my leg. Your love has no ending, he says in his four-year-old voice, and A's eyes fill with tears.

On the couch in the living room downstairs, we start a movie. Friends do this, don't they? When their husbands are out of town, friends share dinner and a movie, right? And don't some of them sit close like this? My head on her lap, her hands in my hair, Angels in America on the screen, our hands so close I feel the electricity. Our fingertips touch, trace lines, the angel on the screen in sepia light, the intertwining of fingers, fingertips following lines onto palms, wanting lines on palms—the credits roll. A springs up suddenly from the couch, flips on all the lights, takes a deep breath. You should go. At the doorway, we are too close. You should go.

Two weeks later, we tell our husbands we are going out to dinner together but actually we drive to a dark beach, build a fire in the shelter there, and read our Christmas gifts to each other: vignettes we have each written about the past year. We are both English teachers, but we miss what we are saying to each other in lines like your slender fingers on the neck of my guitar and you are a tidal pool I want to explore. A's husband understands, then finds her vignettes on their computer, orders us to stop.

But. In the middle of that night, we email longing to each other. I recognize I have never felt such desire for my husband, who watches me with worried looks at dinner, but I do not understand. I do not speak this language, and neither does A.

March 2005. Friends invite A and me to backpack to a glacial lake and the cabin there, and we go. Maybe if we had been honest with ourselves, we would have admitted we hoped for—we did not know what we hoped for. After hours of star-gazing, our two friends finally tire and disappear into the cabin to go to sleep, but A and I stay at the fire, and she moves to sit behind me and I lean against her and at some moment beneath the stars I tip my head back and she says she wants to kiss me and I tell her yes. We are awkward, adolescent, teeth knocking teeth, but I have never touched such soft lips, my tongue tracing hers, my fingertips at her jawline. We shouldn't be doing this. One of us or both of us say it, we both know it. We rise, intending to ensconce ourselves safely in the cabin with our friends, but on the cabin deck A turns me toward her, and this kiss contains fire.

June 2005. For two months, in coded notes, in secret meetings at trailheads, we try to put it all away. We are both married. This is wrong. We shouldn't be doing this. A's husband is right to forbid this. It endangers our marriages. But then the sun emerges from the clouds in June and the sky is so blue, and we summit mountains together, ride our bikes along the ocean in the warm wind, chase her children along the sandy beach, forget the risk. Somehow, A convinces her husband we have "moved our friendship to a safe place," and he agrees she can go on a backpacking trip with me in the Yukon. I can't remember what my husband says.

The Yukon. We put her car on the ferry, take the ferry from Juneau to Haines, then drive north to the Canadian border. Later, we joke that the literal border crossing gave us permission to cross other borders. At first, it just feels good to be free of supervision. She drives, I play silly songs on my guitar in the passenger seat, we eat raspberries. We set up camp on the shore of the vast Kluane Lake, walk the beach looking for driftwood so we can build a fire.

It isn't until the early morning, in the filtered yellow light of the tent, that we turn to each other in our sleeping bags and kiss. Softly, at first, like before, tender, sweet, innocent, tracing each other's faces with fingertips. But then we begin to learn the language, discover heat, hunger, need. I want her in my bones, I want to breathe her breath and still we are just kissing, but it is a kind of kissing I have never imagined and I know she has never imagined either. For hours, we do not speak words, but trace poems onto each other's jawlines, collarbones, lips.

Then we hike. Somehow, we force ourselves to emerge from the tent, to pack up, to drive to the Slims River trailhead and hike, and it is as if our morning hours in the tent did not occur. We don't talk about it. We separate ourselves from the two women in the tent, because it was holy, what happened, but also because we are terrified. Hiking, A and I are best friends as usual, joking, helping each other cross glacial streams, yelling "Hey, bear!" to discourage a grizzly from coming closer to our lunch spot. Fifteen miles later, we trudge into the backcountry camping spot at Canada Creek, exhausted, grinning. We drink orange Tang with vodka, eat our Ramen noodles, and then fall into our tent and sleep. And we wake, in the glowing sunlight of a Yukon night, and find each other again, more passionately this time, urgent, I want to weep at this much tenderness, I want to live here with her against her warm bare skin forever.

No guilt or regret intrudes in that space between us in the Yukon wilderness. Hike by day, map each other's bodies by night. I recognize her; I have been searching for her. When we touch, we have come home at last, finally content.

It's not until we drive back into town, that the world names what we have done betrayal. A calls her family and when she returns to where I sit at a roadside diner, her eyes carry the weight of what we have done.

The day after we return from the Yukon, we meet on a secluded rocky beach in Juneau. In my journal, we take turns trying to put the Yukon into words, and we fail because it is in our bodies, and cannot be translated. Then we hold each other and weep, because we have decided to put this away forever.

She has decided. I can't. I have visited a country I never knew existed, and it is a country in which I want to live. Every night I lie beside my husband and wish he were a woman. No. I wish he were A.

On the phone, I tell my friend Ann the entire story. Ann came out in college, and she lives in New York with her partner, Marie. Sarah, she says, is it possible you've discovered you are lesbian?

I burst into tears. Lesbian? No! I'm married—I've got long hair! Silence from Ann, then a gentle, So do I.

For the entire summer, I don't hear from A. She doesn't stop by randomly or leave secret messages for me anywhere. But on the top of a mountain, I tell my husband the entire story and then, in tears, I confess to him and to myself, I think I've discovered I love women, and because he is good and because he loves me, he says through his own tears, I know, I've begun to know, and he pulls me into his arms and holds me a long time.

We read books together, he and I, case studies of married women who discover they are gay. It is 2005. Brokeback Mountain is showing in the movie theaters, and Ellen DeGeneres has been out and proud for several years, and of course there's the Indigo Girls, but it's also been less than a decade since Matthew Shepard was murdered in Laramie and "Don't Ask, Don't Tell" is the active rule in the military and only the state of Massachusetts allows gay marriage. Add to that my upbringing in socially conservative Iowa, and I am afraid. Sad, and afraid.

My husband and I decide to separate. At the end of the summer of 2005, he travels to South America and I stay in Alaska. Can a kiss do so much damage? I had still never made love with a woman. A and I hadn't crossed that boundary, though I wanted to in the Yukon. She said it was our husbands' territory. But see, this is evidence that my identity as a lesbian was never defined merely by sexual desire, but by my desire for a full self.

Fall 2005. I live alone for the first time in my life. I travel to New York to stay with Sarah and Marie, search bookstores for lesbian stories, search sidewalks for lesbian lives. I ask what it means to be this new self. Sarah and Marie inhabit a world I never noticed before. How do I gain membership? What are the rules? I read and read, but only Adrienne Rich's poetry gives me answers: our stories are not in any of the books.

I don't remember how it happens, but in late September A visits me late at night after her hockey game. She looks haunted, desperate. He says I should explore this. I should figure out if it's really what I want. And that's why we find ourselves hiking to another cabin one Saturday night in the rain, bottles of wine in our backpacks because we both know without discussing it that this night we will travel the entire territory, and maybe we will need some help from alcohol to be brave enough.

We are barely in view of the cabin when we reach for each other hungrily, needing each other's skin, taste. . . . Throwing our backpacks inside the cabin, the wine forgotten, we are up against the wall, clothes shed, ripped, our hands on each other's body, bare skin, our mouths tracing every contour with our tongues, we slide to the floor and find each other there, and we cannot be satiated, for hours, we lose ourselves in our lovemaking.

At some point in the night, we pause for breath, step out onto the deck. She stands behind me, her arms around my belly, our naked skin warm where we touch each other, but the night wind is cool on our faces. Above us, a sky full of stars and the green ribbons of the Northern Lights. The approval of the universe.

The next afternoon, I sit alone on my bed examining the bruises on my hips, my skinned knees, my raw nipples. I touch my sore mouth, feel my swollen tongue. And I am certain of two truths: I am a woman who loves women, and I do have a soul mate in this world.

Our night at the cabin is the deciding factor for A. She moves out into a tiny rental house that slants and has moss growing on the walls. The kids think it's an adventure to live there half of each week. Her husband throws her belongings onto the lawn, shouts anger into the phone, refuses to hear her decision as a discovery of sexuality, accuses her of betrayal, adultery. Because she is afraid of him and afraid for her reputation, she hides the fact of me, and we meet only in darkness: in the slanty house after the kids are asleep, in my apartment on the nights the kids are with their father, far out the road by the ocean, at secluded picnic areas. We never sleep. We make love, and make love, and learn each other's bodies and then experiment to learn more.

At Christmas, we again read each other vignettes we've written about the previous year. Our annual gift to each other is the story we cannot find.

By day, for over a year, we are merely best friends, two public school English teachers who have separated from their husbands, so of course need each other's company.

Fall 2006. I think. The dates begin to blur here. Two divorces finalized. A buys a house. We continue our two lives, the publicly acceptable one and the hidden one. Enviously, I watch couples who live openly; I discover Jeanette Winterson's books; I find movies like Fire and Tipping the Velvet. A says she isn't sure she's lesbian, that she just loves me. She doesn't really want to discuss it.

We wear matching silver rings with "all my life" inscribed inside. I wear mine on my wedding ring finger. She wears hers on her right hand.

Again, at Christmas, we read each other what we've written about our love. She says my writing this year sounds sad. Hers sounds heavy.

Spring 2007. We escape Juneau for a week, travel to San Francisco. Of course. We feel like we have learned a foreign language no one around us speaks, we know two other lesbian couples in town, but they have been together for decades and besides they can live openly. (Why can't we live openly? Who can tell us how to live in this country we've discovered?) The moment we step off the plane in San Francisco, A takes my hand in hers, and my heart beats faster. It's daylight, a crowded airport, and here she is acknowledging to the world that we are together. Her first public admission.

Shyly, we enter a lesbian bar, play "Apples to Apples" with the bartender, share drinks in a corner thinking every woman there recognizes us as imposters. We visit sex toy stores, pick up purple glittery dildos, laugh to imagine wearing pink feather fringe on our underwear. Mostly, we drive the curves of Highway 1 and make love in California's free air.

Our trips out of Juneau become our real life. No angry sad ex-husbands, no guilt about custody arrangements, no fear that someone will discover we are together, no weight. A carries all of this, so I carry her out of Juneau again in the summer of 2007 to Mexico.

Tulum. The white sand beach and a language we can speak enough to ask for a private cabana with a view of the ocean. A thunderstorm over the sea in the darkness, and we make love in a bed suspended from the ceiling, our bodies hidden by white netting. Another day, we rent a motorbike and speed along the turquoise sea, find a beachside bar with hammocks, make love on our hammock in the darkness. We race up the steps of a Mayan temple, and I think the hieroglyphics tell us secrets.

Christmas 2007. A says, Maybe you should move in? I've waited. Finally. Yes. I'd love to.

Life doesn't move at the correct speed. Now my furniture and my clothing live in her house, and her children nestle close to me at bedtime to hear a story, and it seems we have achieved the life we want. Months before, I applied to adopt a child from Ethiopia. Now people in our town congratulate A on the coming addition to "our" family. We have nothing to fear.

Except our bodies. We should always fear our bodies. That spring of 2008, A suddenly gains sixty pounds, becomes chronically tired, her joints ache and flash with pain, her heart beats irregularly. She visits four different doctors and gets four different opinions. No one knows what's wrong. At the beginning of the summer, the two of us travel to Jasper and Banff in the Canadian Rockies, and A is in so much pain she thinks we'll have to go home.

But then the pain disappears. We kayak, mountain bike, hike, make love in our tent and in train bathrooms, write in our journals beside each other. See? We have found the life we want. A has moved her silver ring to her wedding ring finger.

Together, we bring home a toddler from Ethiopia. Our house is raucous and playful, three kids, the two of us turning up the music for random dance parties, inviting the neighborhood to join us. Here, here, we endured so much sadness to reach this life, and here we are, out, two women sharing a life together raising children. It is a true story and it can be told.

What happens? My memory is clouded by diapers and crying in the night and tea parties, soccer games and sleepovers and my own lesson plans and A's attempts to finish work on a PhD. Sometimes, we seem to exist in different lives, and then find each other in the darkness. Other times, we sit in our kitchen happily surrounded by the chaos of our family. In the summer of 2009, we take our family to Colorado, and it's true that sometimes she seems distant, but I have heard this is how it is to be a spouse of a PhD candidate, and I play with the children. One night, when they are asleep, A and I drag a mattress to the deck and make love while thunder reverberates against the mountains, our skin illuminated by lightning flash. The raindrops cool our skin after. In the morning, we make breakfast for the kids and grin at each other. This is the life we wanted, this is the life we wanted.

What happens? Our days are transporting kids to activities in our red mini-van, grading papers, grocery-shopping, taking the recycling to the city bins, cleaning the house, fixing the house. And? It's not that we become reduced but that we become subsumed. Or that I forget to pay attention. I think I close my eyes too long. When I open them, it is the spring of 2010, and A is irritable. She has gained more weight, and her skin is oddly thin, she bleeds easily, she bruises at my slightest touch, at her neck is a mysterious hump, her hair loses its luster and becomes stringy. She is worse than irritable. Often, she is mean.

But in the darkness, in our bedroom? Our bodies never forget each other.

What happens? I take our youngest to the Midwest to visit my mother for a month. On the phone, A wakes up. I'm sorry. I AM in here. I've just been stressed. At my sister's wedding in Colorado, A and I dance and her arms feel good and strong around me. Then, in the fall of 2010, a good friend of ours dies suddenly, and we are asked to organize the memorial. For days, we stay up late together choosing music and photographs, laughing at memories, holding each other when we cry. Everything will be okay.

What happens? She forgets to be okay. She leaves? Her body is in our house, but she is not in her body. When I look into her eyes, they are empty, and that terrifies me. Her voice sharpens, she does not want to stop moving to have time with us, she no longer notices our youngest child, she has lost all her softness. She is a stranger.

A therapist tells me I am in an unhealthy relationship. She says I sound like the wife of an alcoholic. She says, Every time you say she'll change, you know she probably won't, right? But the therapist doesn't know that the problem is I live with a stranger. A has gotten lost somewhere and can't find her body. The therapist is right, though, that I can't live with this person. It's become dangerous.

Christmas 2010. We do not share our writing with each other, though we have both written it. Mine is sad, pleading, angry. Hers is confused (I read it later).

January 2011: I tell her I need to leave for awhile, probably in May when the school year ends.

But at random times that spring, she returns. She is playful, loving, attentive, and I think that what has broken in her has been fixed, but then she'll rage, or descend into catatonic sadness. Our house embodies whatever is happening to her. The pipes freeze and burst in the ceilings, and the entire living room ceiling falls in jagged chunks of plaster and old rotten newspaper. I hide the knives when she begins to say people are following her. I cannot breathe. And yet one day we snowshoe up to a frozen lake and it feels good to be with her for the entire day in the sunshine. On a weekend in May, we hike in to a cabin and invent a dialogue between a backwoods man and woman, laughing the entire time. But we do not make love that night. I hold her, but she seems too fragile for more. When she flickers back into life, I am afraid to disturb her, afraid her eyes will empty again.

I am too afraid. I am responsible for my daughter, whom I now think of only as mine. I believe, or let myself believe, that if I leave for a while A will be jolted back into herself. I believe we have time.

June 2011. I leave. I tell A I need a break for a couple of months, that I'm taking my daughter with me to Colorado where my sister lives, that after August 1, we can start writing letters again, see if we can find our way back to each other.

Because I don't tell anyone why I am leaving, when people in our town find A wandering confused, bleeding, then lying on the floor of her classroom unconscious they assume it is deep grief at a lover's betrayal. Later, the doctors will say she had a seizure, but they will not be able to say why. Later, when her delusions return, the doctors will not be able to explain that, either.

What happens? In Colorado, I mourn her. Where has the woman I love gone?

We exchange letters in August and September, and she is there in her familiar handwriting, in the way she never completes the curve of her "a", the way "ing" is a scribbled line. Her words are poetry, and they draw me back to her. I decide I was wrong to leave.

And then.

And then: she dies.

I drive home from Denver on a Saturday night in October 2011 knowing I have two text messages from Alaskan friends, call ASAP, and the Big Dipper spans the entire sky, and somehow I know.

She has died. A has died.

She is 42, and I am 34, the age she was the first day we met.

The autopsy offers no answers except that the cause of death was an enlarged heart, which I understand in my poet brain but which makes no sense to the doctors. I fly to Alaska, and I wander through our house and she is not there. Her children and I walk along the beach together and she is not there. When I hike to the place at the top of the dam where we exchanged our silver rings, and try to will the October air to freeze me to death, she is not there, either.

It is only the night I come back to Colorado that I find her. The front door of my rental house slams and I sit up in my bed, and there she is, standing in the living room holding a suitcase in each hand, grinning at me, her dark curly hair covered in snow. I am so glad to see her. Comforted, I lie down again and drift into dreams where the two of us walk hand in hand through foreign cities that smell of cinnamon.

When I wake in the morning, I see the slam had not been the front door, but a cottonwood tree that collapsed under the weight of snow and crushed my car.

A is not here.

For a year and a half, I descend to a dark place I never thought I would go. I am Orpheus seeking Eurydice and sometimes I glimpse her but then she fades into a grey distance and I have to keep wandering, calling. I don't want to return to the land of light. Let me stay down here. Let me fade, too.

Summer 2013. I carry A's ashes in a Ziplock bag in my backpack, and I also carry a large round river stone on which I have had her name carved. I fly to Juneau, where I leave my child with friends, and then I take the ferry to Haines, rent a car, drive into the Yukon. I camp alone in a tent that filters the sunlight onto my bare skin.

I climb to an alpine ridge that overlooks the Slims River and the Kaskawulsh Glacier. Here, I am insignificant. So is A, so is our love. The mountains rise ancient on all sides of me, and the glacier says time does not move as human beings believe it does. What is ten years? Whitman: what is less or more than a touch?

I nestle the stone beside purple and yellow wildflowers, and I speak Walt's words like a prayer before I reach into the Ziplock bag. I, too, am untranslatable. It is not truly ash, but grit and fragment of bone. I wanted to be in her bones. When I taste my fingers, I taste salt. I open my hand. The wind changes direction, blows the ashes into my eyes and my nose and my mouth, and I have to laugh. I can hear A laughing, light-hearted A, healthy A, free in the air and in the soil.

I release handful after handful of her ashes until the bag is empty and I lower myself to the ground and weep.

A soft breeze caresses my cheek, plays with my hair. For a moment, I glimpse the two of us walking along the river trail in the glacial plain below, in the sunshine of eight years ago, and I know I will not lose her completely until my own body becomes ash and fragments of bone, too. But memory is only partial solace.

What has happened?

Now, at night, when I climb into my bed alone, I imagine for a moment I hear her soft breathing, I allow myself to think I could reach out and lay my hand on her hip. I still sleep on my side of the bed.

At the beginning, we used to say in awe that Something beyond us guided us toward each other. I can't think about what our ending means, then. But I can write. I'll write you into my fiction, A, and I'll love you again and again there. I'll tell the stories we couldn't find. I'll reach for you, and if I miss you one place, I'll search another.

Jan O'Connor

Jan O'Connor has an MA in English from St. Louis University and an MFA in Theatre from Southern Illinois University, Carbondale. She has directed more than fifty plays and musicals in theatres on both coasts and in the Midwest, is a member of Dramatists Guild and the International Centre for Women Playwrights, and serves as vice-chair of Alliance of Los Angeles Playwrights.

Interview

I.B. Why do you write?

J.O. I write to try to work out - for my own sake - some way to deal with what appear to be life's unknowable mysteries and relentless contradictions.

I.B. If you were a book, what book would you be? Why?

J.O. The Bible. Because then I'd either know the answers to almost everything or have written the most amazing mythology ever.

I.B. Do you consider yourself a feminist? If so, how do YOU define feminism?

J.O. I suppose I am and what feminism means for me is valuing what women have to offer more than what men do.

I.B. Share something interesting about yourself that has nothing to do with writing/publishing.

J.O. I love movies, especially the classics of any era, and I feel I can be great good friends, maybe even a soulmate, with anybody who's ten favorite movies list would match mine.

I.B. You have been given an opportunity to write the last sentence you will ever write. What is that sentence?

J.O. "Since it's only mediocre people who are always at their best, at least I wasn't mediocre."

Case of Arrested Development

I was already thirty years old, and had been married and divorced before I ever felt the stirrings of desire for another woman. The notion had simply never occurred to me. Raised in a strict Catholic family in an insular Italian neighborhood in Brooklyn, I'd always been told that with my dark eyes, long curly hair and short stature I was made for marriage and motherhood. I'd tried the marriage part, which didn't work out. Then I'd gone to college to get a degree in English, because teaching, as even my parents grudgingly admitted, was "something to fall back on" if I insisted on becoming an old maid.

And that's how I came to find myself teaching high school English in the rarified atmosphere of an extremely wealthy community in bucolic upstate New York. Called Verdant Hills, it was the sort of town so enamored of itself that the local boutiques sold glittery T-shirts reading: "London…Paris…Verdant Hills." Being from Brooklyn, I'd never known these kinds of places existed. So I knew I was fortunate and was grateful to get the job, which probably happened because I cheerfully agreed to teach English and direct the school's annual plays. The first one scheduled was South Pacific, and, as a town with money to burn, Verdant Hills spared no expense for sets and costumes. They even imported live frangipani for Emil's plantation. Best of all, they provided a local dance instructor as choreographer. That was Sandy, a gorgeous blond with long thick hair, large breasts, a tiny waist and powerful legs.

She was one-half of what the town considered its cutest couple. Her husband, Eric, a local realtor, was equally gorgeous. But what I appreciated even more than their beauty was that they readily welcomed me, inviting me to dinner, and treating me as if I actually belonged in that community. And even though the town pretty much looked on teachers as the hired help, Sandy and Eric had gotten me invited to a party hosted by the parents of one of the not-very-talented students I diplomatically cast in a major role in South Pacific.

The parents' home was an enormous Tudor mansion near a lake, and the event, just one of their many parties for Verdant Hills' 100 finest citizens, happened to be "informal." That meant it was in the afternoon. Everyone came casually but expensively dressed, the catering was buffet-style with tables laden with hors d'oeuvres and desserts. The professionally staffed bars were scattered here and there in the main hall and library.

I launched myself into this rarified atmosphere wearing my freshly purchased, casual Ann Taylor dress (bought in a nearby town on sale). I tried to relax and make small talk with people who expected a lot and judged quickly, but even my second gin and tonic wasn't helping much. Then I spotted Eric and with a rush of relief I made a beeline over to him.

Here was someone safe, someone I could be myself around. Maybe he felt the same way because he gave me a smile, leaned in and whispered: "What do you say Sandy and me and you get together and fuck each others' brains out?"

As I sputtered some of the gin and tonic back into my glass, Eric laughed and started talking about something else. I had no idea what it was, but I wrapped both my hands around my glass, took a big swig, nodded my head and laughed too. Then someone else got his attention and he moved away toward the library.

Things got a little fuzzy for me after that, but at some point I found myself standing next to Sandy at the dessert table. It seemed I had yet another drink in my hand, so I chuckled and said to her: "Eric thinks we should all get together and fuck each others' brains out." Without a second's hesitation, Sandy breathed, "Who needs Eric?" and began kissing me, on my neck and my throat, and my cheek, her pillow lips warm and silky and purposeful, her scent intoxicating. I thought I might faint. Or burst into flames. Or just die of sheer ecstasy. But somehow I came to and pulled away from her as I laughed and gave her a friendly hug. My god, we were surrounded by a hundred people. A hundred Verdant Hills people. Someone must have seen this moment of illicit, electric contact. I waited for outraged cries to drive me in disgrace from the Tudor stronghold, putting a shameful end to my now-disastrous teaching career forever. But I heard no outraged cries. Only party chatter and the clink of silverware and glasses. I looked around cautiously. People were talking and laughing and eating and drinking, and nobody was looking at Sandy and me. When I turned to her, she just smiled sweetly, popped a chocolate-covered strawberry in her beautiful mouth and drifted away.

After a few seconds, I managed to pick up one of those strawberries myself and head stiffly to one of the powder rooms. Inside I locked the door and stared into the mirror. I looked the same. But I felt transformed. I touched the places on my neck and throat and cheek where Sandy had kissed me. They were warm; they throbbed. And that's when I realized I wanted this girl, this gorgeous woman with her thick hair and soft breasts and long legs. I wanted to caress her, every bit of her, outside and inside. And I wanted her to kiss me and touch me everywhere, all the time. How could I have been blind all my life to these feelings that now overwhelmed me? And what could I possibly do about them? Oh, I knew what I wanted to do. I wanted to throw open the bathroom door, race across the floor to Sandy, pick her up and carry her off to paradise.

Instead, I turned on the tap and splashed my burning face with cold running water. I took deep breaths to slow my racing heart. Then I stared at myself in the mirror and knew it was impossible. I had a certain kind of life. I was a teacher with an obligation to be a role model for these children and their formidable parents. I had to be, above all, beyond reproach. I squeezed my eyes shut.

Just then someone knocked loudly on the door and, in that instant, I felt as if a cold wind was blowing me back on course. I had no idea what to do about Sandy, but I couldn't hide in the powder room any longer. Setting my face into a tight smile, I opened the door. There stood the daughter of my hosts, the no-talent girl I'd reluctantly cast in South Pacific. She was beaming at me, thanking me again for casting her and wanting to be sure I met her parents. As she dragged me across the room to them, I glanced around nervously for Sandy or Eric but didn't spot them. Hoping the coast was clear, I gushed my thanks to my hosts and then murmured something about having to get home. Many, many papers still to correct. And so I made my cowardly escape.

The next rehearsal for South Pacific was a few days later and by then I had brought myself back under control. When I saw Sandy, she looked at me, shyly and expectantly, but I gave her my best blank stare. My message was clear. Too dangerous, too scary, too soon, too impossible.

So we never spoke of that moment at the party. Not then and not during the two long years I lived and worked in the ridiculous town of Verdant Hills. I'd convinced myself that I'd only dreamed it. Until it happened again, in a different place, at a different time, and with a different woman.

Sarah Lyn Rogers

Sarah Lyn Rogers is an MFA student at San José State University, where her emphases are fiction and poetry. She is interested in exploring gender, identity (sexual and otherwise), and communication in her work. When she is not writing, she is an assistant fiction editor for *The Rumpus*. She also works as a writing mentor, copyeditor, and layout manager for Society of Young Inklings, a nonprofit writing community and publishing imprint for young writers.

Interview

I.B. Why do you write?

S.R. I write because words run through my blood. I've kept a journal since age eight and I stumbled into poetry as a young teen. These pursuits feel natural to me. I like visual art, too, but that process is a frustrating one, even when I like the end product. With writing, there is doubt, but never a sense that *maybe I can't do this*.

I.B. If you were a book, what book would you be? Why?

S.R. If I were a book, I would love to be a book on writing, like *Writing Down the Bones* by Natalie Goldberg, or *Bird by Bird* by Anne Lamott. These pieces are instructive and touching because they are the perfect hodgepodge of memoir, self-help, how-to, and even philosophy (Natalie Goldberg's process is informed by Zen meditation, Anne Lamott's by gentleness with the self—she has an inspirational chapter called "Shitty First Drafts"). I like how these manuals are general, intended for anyone, but they're specifically about the author's patterns of understanding the world.

I.B. Do you consider yourself a feminist? If so, how do YOU define feminism? If not, still explain your understanding of feminism.

S.R. I feel like we need a new label for persons who believe in treating humans equally and without superficial judgment. I hesitate to align myself with the label of "feminist" (although I strive for equal treatment, fairness, and accountability in my everyday dealings with people) because I have often seen this label used as an excuse for mudslinging rather than an opportunity for dialogue. I think women (all people, really) should be free to express their appearance however they want (Don't shave? That's fine! Wear heavy makeup? That's fine, too!), to have a profession that makes them happy (being a stay-at-home mom is just as cool as being a high-power CEO if that's what you choose), and to feel safe and confident in their relationships and environments. It saddens me that both male feminists and masculists are vilified on the internet (I'm looking at you, Tumblr). I know there are always exceptions, that not everyone's intentions are good, but the assumption that men can't fight for our rights, and that men can't raise awareness for their own issues, is just as unfair an ideology as the patriarchy we are all struggling to dismantle. Generalizations about groups of people are unfair—they are something that we as feminists are purporting to battle. The fight for equality should not be "us" versus "them," because the construction of an Other is harmful and unfair; the fight should be us AND them.

I.B. Share something interesting about yourself that has nothing to do with writing/publishing.

S.R. I play drums, sing backing vocals, and paint album art and promotional materials for a San Francisco Bay Area band called Elflock. I'm in the process of hand-drawing several hundred frames for an animated music video set for release this summer. You can check out our music at: http://elflockmusic.bandcamp.com/

I.B. You have been given an opportunity to write the last sentence you will ever write. What is that sentence?

S.R. I never learned how to read.

Little Red and the Elf Princess

On the first day, Red said nothing.

She was used to that. On a day lacking any foreshadowing, Red had stepped out of her tiny cottage in the woods to walk the dirt trail into town, aching with thirst for the chai concentrate that her jerk housemates had finished without her permission. The jerks. She planned to hide the replacement purchase at the back of the fridge, behind the kale, where ravenous men of twenty-something, that magical age, were unlikely to look.

Birds chirped, the sun shone, and everything around her seemed alive with promise. "You get that chai, girl!" the wind seemed to say. Nothing prepared her for the curse.

Halfway into town, at the fork in the road, there was a tree that Red had not seen before —white and split down the middle into two trunks, which twisted around each other like spineless lovers. It had black leaves and was as unsettling as it was beautiful. Resting against the base of the trunk was an old beggar woman with a serious case of crazy-eyes. Red took a nervous breath and played her usually-trusty game of I-don't-see-you, averting her gaze from the bedraggled figure and hoping to pass without being accosted.

No such luck. With a creepy stare, the beggar woman shook her enchanted coffee can and muttered the following incantation: Spare some change, Miss?

Red paused, knowing that she only ever carried plastic, and not knowing that she was about to suffer the consequences of committing the most infamous fairy tale faux pas: snubbing a mysterious old lady in the woods. Her mouth felt dry as she continued the ritual exchange with a shrug and a "Sorry."

"Have a nice day."

With these powerful words, the beggar woman cursed Red, laughing evilly to herself before hacking a disgusting wet cough that would compel even the kindest of souls to vacate. Red was confused, and definitely grossed out.

"You, too. Bitch," Red replied, surprising herself. It was the wrong thing to say.

When she got to Ye Olde Goodly Marketplace, which had a cringe-worthy name but was the only grocery store walking distance from her house, Red couldn't find the right words for any of the customary social interactions forced upon her in public places like these.

In the aisle for "SpecialTeas from the Orient," (Gross, Red always thought), Red spotted her coveted chai on the tippy-top shelf. She stood on her tippy-toes to grab the box, stretched her arm, and flipped her small hand around, hoping to knock the item down and catch it in her checkered A-line skirt—a nice, broad target, like the trampoline below suicide jumpers.

She might have been able to reach it if she had actually gone through with the ballet classes her parents had suggested to her as a child. But Red was both introverted and clumsy, two strikes against her now, so she never learned to stand en pointe. She had to flag an employee.

A smiling young man in the Marketplace uniform—loose-fitting white pirate shirt tucked into brown knickerbockers—saw Red's attempt at independence and rushed to rescue her from her womanish weakness. Still smiling, he stretched his tall frame only the slightest bit, and came at the box with his hand open like the claw in a glass box of stuffed animals. He crouched down patronizingly and patted Red on the head when he handed the box to her.

"Thanks, asshole."

Oh her god.

The employee looked confused, and a little hurt, before shaking his head and fleeing the aisle to aid kinder distressing damsels.

Red did not speak to anyone in line at the register, afraid of offending strangers she would likely never see again. But it was hard to avoid a direct question from the checker.

"Paper or plastic?"

"Coach," Red replied, making an apologetic face.

"I'm sorry?"

Yeah, I am too, she thought, and could do nothing.

"Or Luis Vuitton." Red's eyes widened, betraying her embarrassment, but she kept talking, hoping that everyone would think she had a weird sense of humor. Someone, or something, did, but she had no control over her own strange words. "No? Hmph!"

Her eyes, now frantic, darted to the exit. Red made an I-don't-know gesture, palms up in penitence, and grabbed the chai as she speed-walked out of the store. She did not turn around.

On the walk back to her cottage, Red tried to piece together her unsettling afternoon. Unsettling, like the twisty tree. What was different about today? she wondered. She remembered the old woman at the fork in the path and walked faster toward it, hoping to sort out whatever had happened to her there, during a seemingly routine interaction earlier. She could offer to buy food for the woman, suffering the embarrassment of the Goodly Marketplace once more. She could even hand over her credit card. I can call the bank and cancel it any time, she thought. Just please, please fix me.

When she got to the fork, the woman and the tree were gone. Red scanned the surrounding woods, hoping to spy a lump of tattered black clothing, but she was completely alone. She walked the rest of the way home, slowly now, as the sun sank pinkly behind the silhouettes of trees. She hoped to make it back before night, but, honestly, she hardly cared about anything now.

As the last of the pixelated purple sky darkened, Red opened the front door of her quaint cottage. Her housemates three were on the couch, smashing each other with cartoon mallets, lost in their video game world. Red meant to slip unnoticed down the hall to her room and sleep away whatever weirdness had been thrust upon her, but she got no further than the doorway before her mouth opened.

"Alright, you motherfuckers. I want everyone out."

Everyone dropped a controller with a plasticky thud and turned to look at her. The game world increased in entropy along with Red's real life. She made a mortified face, and her hand flew to her mouth as if to shove the words back inside, but the damage was done.

The first housemate opened his mouth to speak, then shut it again.

The second housemate opened his mouth to speak, furrowed his brow, and sighed loudly.

The third housemate was wily. He clenched one fist and said, "What the hell, dude? Seriously?!"

Red opened her mouth to speak, then shut it again. Hesitantly, she spoke.

"What's the matter, pretty boy? Not man enough for a fight?"

Not the words she wanted at all.

The third housemate's face burned with rage as Red fled down the hall, hair flying cape-like in her haste.

Once in her room, Red flopped onto her bed and pulled her journal from the drawer in her bedside table. She dug deeper into the drawer, feeling for her favorite pen, hoping it would bring her luck. On the lined pages, she swirled cowardly curlicues before attempting to write. She was afraid to discover whose voice could be channeled through her pen.

Something is wrong with me.

So far, her own.

Today? From now on? I don't know how to describe it except that the only words I can say are the wrong words. Not even words that I secretly WANT to say… just… things that are completely inappropriate and which hurt and confuse others. I don't know why, and I don't know how long it will last. I am so sorry to everyone I've addressed.

It wasn't much, but being able to speak truthfully in writing meant that Red wasn't confined to her own head. She tore out the page and hurried it to the kitchen, where she could stick it onto the refrigerator for everyone to see and understand.

She walked softly, but dishes in the sink settled with a clatter, sharply directing a trio of glances from the television to Red. Everyone gave her their pissiest faces before turning purposefully back to the TV. Red didn't care. She knew that everyone would see her note and realize that she hadn't meant what she'd said.

The morning was uncharacteristically bright in the cottage. For a moment, Red couldn't place why. Not until she stared out the living room window at the early sun and the trees.

Where were the curtains? The game console and controllers were gone with the TV. A peek in each cabinet was like looking into a cave. All of the dishes were taken, except for the dirty ones in the sink.

Feeling like Goldilocks in her own home, Red opened her first housemate's bedroom door. Bright. Curtainless. Drawers open, everything empty, everything gone but the heavy furniture. The place looked ransacked, but it wasn't by thieves. Housemates number two and three had also stolen away. The house felt too big and too small. Nothing was right.

By the sink, Red's note was crumpled into an angry ball.

* * *

Red fell into a routine. Her ailment was easy to manage if she simply did not speak to anyone. She wondered whether she would get the reputation of a witch, holed up in her cottage in the woods, never speaking, no evidence of her presence except for the lights in her house and occasional sightings. Maybe the rumor would be that the cottage was haunted, and no one really lived there. She felt like no one, so that was appropriate.

The transition was strange at first. She wrote a letter to her parents, professing that to be more connected to the real world (that was a laugh), she'd sworn off modern technology and would no longer be using her television, her phone, or her computer. The first two were truths. Red never bothered to replace the TV, and she was too afraid to use the phone anymore, so she canceled her service. The computer was a lie; she copyedited manuscripts for a living. She'd had to up the ante to pay the mortgage on her storybook cottage with no housemates around, not even dwarves to help her with chores, har har. But it's easy to churn out manuscripts quickly when one has no social life.

Red's parents were surprisingly gung-ho about her decision to live "off-the-grid," as her hippie dad would say. Once the logistics of her silence were explained away, it was easier for Red to adapt to her new, somber life as a mute observer, without the humorous mood which had previously colored her outlook on everything. Wanting to muffle the inner chatter of her anguish, Red turned her gaze outward.

On early, early Springtime mornings, she collected wildflowers to press in a book, admiring the sunrise and the chill air, enlivening as any cup of coffee. Wildflowers, sunrises, tiny insects marching purposefully, butterflies (to admire, not to press), grasses waving lazily in the afternoon breeze: Red felt connected to these quiet entities, silent beautiful things which cannot tell you what they mean.

Summer melted blossoms into heavy, golden fruits burdening branches with the weight of their birth, and scorched the grasses into sepia tones. The season was a loud celebration, a self-congratulatory time of harvest and eye-catching colors. Red preferred the quiet dignity of Fall; there were no wildflowers on those mornings, only a fascinating confetti of fallen leaves and crisscrossing congregations of naked branches, both intricate and elegant. The sparseness inspired Red's interest in photography, and she took to carrying a vintage camera in her satchel, where it could bounce around with the pressed flowers of previous seasons and whichever book Red was reading at the time.

One naked Fall morning, Red, with her camera, were in the front yard, just inside the gate, capturing a fat squirrel in a tree silhouetted against the grey morning sky. The comfortable quiet was broken by something Red had not heard for months: a human voice. The voice was lovely—robust, throaty, melodiously working its way through an impromptu song about gardening—and Red was curious to see if its owner's appearance would match.

Red tucked the camera into her satchel and stepped outside of the gate. She pulled the hood of her black cloak over her head to slap the flirty wind away from her neck, and followed the sound of the voice to its origin.

When she thought the singing could not possibly get louder, Red saw another cottage tucked between two redwoods. It was slightly larger than her small house, but it too was surrounded by a low fence. Inside the gate, a young woman was raking leaves. She was tall, wearing a long dress that brushed the toes of her boots. Her long blonde hair fell to her waist. Everything about her looked serene; she had an open, welcoming face. Red thought that she looked like an elf princess… or at least how she imagined an elf princess might look. She approached the cottage and the woman.

On the first day, Red said nothing. She did not have to; she sang.

Red was drawn to the mystery woman who seemed part gypsy, part pioneer woman, part seventies singer-songwriter. But given Red's recent history with words as weapons, she was afraid of what might happen if she spoke. Red felt the double weight of the curse and shy jitters.

Red's nervousness dissolved into tentative action as her voice added itself to the singer's. Red hummed, so softly that only she could hear it at first, plucking pale notes from the air, amazed to hear her own voice as foreign to her as any stranger's.

When was the last time she'd used it? Red used to be someone who apologized to inanimate objects when she would bump into them, sounded her interior monologue while meandering through the house, and enjoyed her echo under bridges and in the hollows of trees. For a short while after her affliction, Red continued these habits, but they always backfired. Crashing into the corner of the counter would now prompt a "Watch it!" rather than the customary "Whoops, sorry." Now when she caught herself muttering during household chores, she heard mean personal attacks about how poorly she was executing them. A well-intentioned shout in places with live acoustics always told her, "Go away!"

So she did. Red retreated to the recesses of her mind and diary, figuring it was better to say nothing than to be forced to listen to herself. She took a much-coaxed and equally-resented vow of silence. It wasn't fair. It felt like a disservice …to young people? …to womankind? to somebody to be seen and not heard, but she supposed it didn't matter when there was no audience.

Despite the wayward ways of her words, Red could still laugh, cry, or sneeze as any normal human could. The latter happened on occasion, but Red did little laughing or crying now that she spent all of her time alone. Nothing moved her to make noise.

Now, beneath the needles of a tree, hovering anxiously outside the gate of a stranger's house, Red was moved. She had not tried singing since that stupid day at the stupid fork. There was no music in her anymore. Or maybe there was, but it needed coaxing—perhaps unknowingly from this stranger, who was kind-looking and hopefully approachable. The woman's simple song seemed magical.

Red felt coaxed. Her harmonizing hums turned into soft *ahs* as she painstakingly parted her chapped lips, still out of sight, hardly noticeable in her black cloak in the shade. To an ordinary person, the sound was dismissible, so subtle that it could have been the wind. The nervous part of Red, which was most of her, hoped that she would be dismissed, so that she could return to her unhappy home and think that she tried to make a change and had failed. But Red knew just by looking at her that the stranger was not ordinary.

The stranger did not ask who was there or stop her lighthearted song. She continued to rake leaves as if she had not heard anything at all, but her eyes searched the neighboring pines. Red's *ahs* increased in volume, encouraged by the stranger's surreptitiousness. Nervous energy shifted to excitement as Red reveled in the opportunity to interact with someone, if nonverbally, then at least audibly, without apparent harm. She felt abuzz with possibilities for the first time in many months, stepping ever so slightly from behind a tree trunk. She didn't want to seem too forward, but she wanted to be seen.

She felt the shock of eye contact. Green. Elf princess eyes, Red thought, magnetic from their gated vantage point fifteen feet away. The stranger's lips curled into a small smile as she stopped singing to ask, "Won't you come in?"

Red peered down the entryway, eyeing the hall's walls, which were a warm butter yellow. The whole house smelled like chamomile. At the end of the hallway was a large mirror, situated such that anyone coming through the front door would watch herself enter the space. Red met her own eyes, curious to view herself from a distance. She looked like a stray cat, not the fancy mystery visitor she had hoped.

On a small end table by the door was a stack of unopened mail next to a thick encyclopedia of folklore, atop which sat a cartoonishly large magnifying glass. Red wondered whether the print was exceptionally tiny, or if her hostess had a flair for the theatrical. The second option seemed likely, considering the pioneer dress. Red smoothed her own black cloak, deciding not to point theatrical fingers. Mounted above the end table were two watercolor paintings of fairies in the night sky, with stars highlighted in gold leaf. The figures faced each other from their separate frames, nearby but in different worlds.

The singer pulled her feet out of her boots before extending her hand and a smile.

"I'm Cecilia. Pleased to make your acquaintance."

Red felt the expectation of niceties in the stranger's smile, but Cecilia radiated no impatience. Red's heart thudded in her ears as hearts always seem to in the most stressful and embarrassing moments. She had not thought about this part; she'd imagined the day passing like a silent film, all cloche hats and killer lipstick and handy frames of text between each interaction. Not wanting to seem rude, and not wanting to speak, either, Red pulled a pen and her pressed flower book from her bag and marred one of its pristine pages to write.

I'm Red. Thank you for inviting me in. I don't talk.

She couldn't pretend to be mute, as she obviously had harnessed her vocal cords in her unconventional introduction. Red watched Cecilia read her spidery handwriting and hoped that she would not have to explain further.

Cecilia pulled the pen from Red's hand.

That's okay. Do you want me to write notes, too?

"...or is it okay if I speak?" she finished, handing the flower book back to Red with another smile.

Red felt teary with relief. She smiled shyly and put the book back into her bag. Cecilia slipped the pen into the pocket of Red's dress.

"Well. I think it's time we had some tea. It's four o'clock somewhere," said Cecilia, with a lazy grin.

As she followed down the hall, Red smiled again and felt a little embarrassed, as if her friendship were too easily won. She imagined tittering behind her hand or a paper fan, a ridiculous Japanese schoolgirl stereotype, which made her smile more. How dumb, Red thought, before deciding not to punish herself for feeling happy.

The kitchen was suffering an identity crisis. White eyelet curtains in the window above the sink upheld the romantic fairy tale décor of the entryway, but in the corner was a red retro booth with a circular chrome table that made Red feel like she was at a fifties diner. She pantomimed popping the collar of a leather jacket and pointed finger-guns at Cecilia, who provided an "eyyy!" with a nod of appreciation.

Cecilia put the kettle on the stove and a collection of sea shanties on her record player. She and Red did the Twist as they waited for the water to boil. Red was surprised about how comfortable she felt with this stranger, and noted that Cecilia looked happy to have company, unless she were simply a naturally happy person, which would be a refreshing change. Cecilia didn't seem to belong to any particular era, which suited Red just fine, as she didn't feel like she belonged to anything.

When the kettle whistled, the two walked to the stove. Cecilia pulled from the cabinet her collections of fresh tea leaves, which looked like magical herbs in their glass jars, and pointed out her favorites: spearmint, peppermint, catmint, and chamomile.

Catmint? Red tapped its jar with her index fingernail, making two tiny pixie sounds. Cecilia poured hot water over their tea selections: catmint and chamomile. The warm chamomile smell of the house, which Red had labeled the Cecilia-scent, was now tinged with cool mint and Red's presence.

At the fifties table, the ladies sipped. Red pulled out her pressed flower book and flipped pages for her new friend. Poppy. Bitterroot. Monkeyflower. Redmaid. Blue witch. Red eyed the elf princess, retrieved the pen from her dress pocket, and flipped to the page on which their earlier exchange was written. She scribbled a hasty self-portrait: stock face, shoulder length hair, short hooded cloak, dress, legs, shoes. Beside mini-her, Red drew a floating crown awaiting a subject. Cecilia obliged, effortlessly sketching herself from the boots up and adding enough detail to her small face that it was recognizably her. She drew an apron on mini-Red and labeled her "Red, maid," referencing the flower. She turned the crown into the gaudy band around a pointed, broad-brimmed hat, labeling herself "Blue, witch" with an inscrutable wink.

After they'd drunk the tea and placed their mugs in the sink with a clink, Cecilia sniffed decisively and said, "Get your shoes."

Red looked puzzled. Cecilia peeked under the table at Red's shoed feet.

"One step ahead, I see. Let's go for a walk."

Cecilia padded down the yellow hall to the front door. Red removed the camera from her bag and snapped a quick shot of Cecilia gracelessly tugging her boots onto her sock-feet.

The pair spent the afternoon and early evening outside, crunching leaves underfoot, gathering a few for Red's dormant collection of pressable plants, looking for woodland creatures both factual and fantastical, releasing plumes of steamy breath, and taking pictures of their surroundings and each other. Cecilia walked Red back to her cottage and indicated "goodbye" with just a finger-waggling wave. The day had passed in near-silence, which was pleasant, and not much unlike the beginning stage of anyone's relationships.

Red spread the developed photographs on her bed. Still reeling from the previous day's successful stint as a human who can interact with exciting, interesting, beautiful humans—well, one human, anyway—she savored each captured moment: Cecilia dangling a leaf above her mouth as if it were an exotic bunch of grapes, three black birds on a white fence, spotted red toadstools, half of Red's face peeping from the hood of her cloak. She couldn't help but notice that the most successful compositions were Cecilia's.

Later, Red wandered again to Cecilia's house, not entirely sure of the way. She had been guided by song yesterday morning, and the walk home was merely the end of a wandering-in-the-woods adventure. The wind was more insistent today, and though it was past noon, the morning grey had not burned to reveal blue sky. Red wrapped her cloak tightly around her and wished for thicker leggings. She took paths that seemed familiar and hoped for the best.

She knew she was close when she heard singing, and there was the house. Red knocked.

Cecilia answered the door with her hair piled in a bun. A splotch of red sauce near the corner of her mouth looked like a beauty mark.

"Come in! I'm making lunch! I wanted something hot to ward off the chilly morning. There's more than enough to share."

Red kicked off her shoes in the entryway and slid down the hall in her socks to the kitchen. Cecilia placed a plate before her. Eggplant parmigiana.

Is she actually magic, or am I the least exciting person ever? Red thought, feeding her inner critic, which had grown immensely since she stopped speaking. She had successfully starved it yesterday, but that only made it voracious for doubt today. The two ate in silence, which was pleasant except for Red's persnickety thoughts.

Red felt a lull in the quiet. Cecilia looked at her as if expecting a response. Red gave her a questioning glance that she hoped indicated that she was sorry for not paying attention.

I can't pantomime all of my thoughts. And it would be so stupid to write everything when she knows I can talk. What am I doing here?

"Are you finished? Let me clear the dishes, and then we'll do something fun."

Breathe. Just let things be. She wants to make this work.

Cecilia led Red to the living room, which looked like a miniature version of an old library, complete with overstuffed armchair, green desk lamps, and a globe that still referred to Czechoslovakia. Red took the armchair. Some small instrument—a lute?—was on an end-table beside it, but Red did not know how to play. Cecilia took her seat behind an honest-to-goodness harp and began to play, looking every bit the caricature of an angel.

Maybe not a caricature, Red thought, as she watched Cecilia's artful fingers flirt with the strings. Lovely.

Cecilia began to sing, and Red hesitantly joined her, with notes but not words, painfully aware of the inconsistent ways in which she commanded her voice. She pulled at frayed threads on the armchair.

When the song ended, a curious expression colored Cecilia's face.

"You can talk…"

Red nodded.

"But you choose not to."

Red nodded again. Anxiety prickled in her veins and tightened the muscles around her jaw.

"Will you let me know why?" Cecilia asked softly.

She looked expectant. Cecilia had seemed so comfortable with the ambiguity yesterday. Curiosity must have gotten the better of her.

Red swallowed.

Cecilia smiled.

"If you want backup, I can supply you with a dictionary and thesaurus," she offered, grinning.

Red took a shaky breath, ready to kick herself. Her heart pounded.

"…A thesaurus: some kind of dinosaur." Oh my god. Shut up.

"Funny!" Cecilia looked pleasantly surprised.

Maybe this will go well after all, Red thought reluctantly.

"Really, though. What's your reason for not talking?" Cecilia pressed on. "I thought maybe it was an interesting getting-to-know-you experiment, but we're friends now. I want to understand."

Please don't make me do this.

"Please. Anything."

Red tried to keep her mouth shut, but it was too late.

"You want to understand. You are everything good. You have everything going for you. And you want the workings of my mind, too. Terrific. Let me help you with that." Red's hands flew to her face. She dug her nails into her scalp.

Cecilia's jaw went slack with shock. She tried to speak, then stopped.

Red stepped toward Cecilia, her palms raised in a silent apology. Cecilia stepped back, shaking her head. Her eyes looked glassy. Red hurriedly gathered her things, flustered and embarrassed. More than that, she was hurt. She was hurtful. How could she harm this person who had done nothing to wrong her? She gave Cecilia a look that said I am not in control, but she didn't know if it would read that way. She ran out the front door, not even stopping for her shoes.

The sky darkened as Red ran. Her socked feet squished through mud, getting poked by the sticks that she trampled. She hardly noticed. Her only goal was escape from that uncomfortable scene, but she could not escape her own voices.

"You knew it would happen. You ruin everything."

That isn't true. I don't do it on purpose.

"You deserve to be alone."

Maybe.

"You certainly don't deserve her."

Does anyone?

"You don't know anything about her! What if she was just pretending to be nice?"

Why would she pretend?

Red's feet felt numb from the cold and the unpaved path. Just as the first fat raindrops began to fall, Red made it back to her cottage, safe from the coming storm but not herself.

"You're not as good as her."

Is anyone? Is she even real? I never deserved her kindness.

"You're not as good as anyone. You'll hurt everyone you let near you."

Red considered that that was true. While she could try to prevent anything like this from happening again by avoiding people forever, she could not undo what she had said tonight. She had to apologize. In writing.

> Cecilia,
>
> You are magical to me. You possess an unearthly beauty, limitless talents, and a genuine kind soul. For these reasons, I consider you superhuman and think of you instead as "elf princess" within the safe space of my mind. I apologize for what I said, and I can offer only this explanation which you are unlikely to believe unless you are truly an elf or a witch (or an extraordinary human): Months ago, for reasons I do not understand, I was cursed by a mysterious old woman in the woods. Yeah. I know. I am only able to speak things which are strange, illogical, mean-spirited, self-deprecating, and beyond my control. I tried to avoid the issue by not talking, but your curiosity was understandable. Would you have believed me if I told you the reason? Could I even have spoken it? I figure it doesn't matter now that I have already damaged our fledgling friendship, but I want to know that I made an effort to explain the unbelievable.
>
> For reasons evident in this letter alone, I should not associate with people, magical or otherwise. Thank you for your many kindnesses. I think it would be best if I stayed away.
>
> ~Red

Red folded the letter and placed it in the pocket of her cloak, where she could hold it before presenting it to the elf princess in the morning, or place it in her mailbox if Cecilia refused to see her. Red would understand. The storm sobbed outside. Red fell onto her bed, crying thick mascara tears onto the sheets.

In the morning, Red's sheets were so spotted with black that they looked like leopard print. Still, she was resolved to do the right thing and resign herself to a solitary life. What was the point of the past two days? To reassure her that it was better to be alone? Red didn't feel sure of anything, except that she wanted to disappear. For everyone else's sake. It was better that way, right?

She wasn't sure.

Red walked through the light rain to Cecilia's cottage, hoping that she would be able to see her, and also hoping that she could simply leave the letter and walk out of her life. She wasn't sure which would hurt less. She knocked.

Cecilia opened the door, her green eyes red-rimmed and concerned.

Red reached her hand into the pocket of her cloak. Her hand was on the letter.

Cecilia searched Red's face for something. She must have found it. She softly cleared her throat and spoke.

"Red—"

Cecilia paused, unsure of what to say. Red waited, hoping she looked as apologetic as she felt. Cecilia took a breath, then smirked a tiny, well-meaning smirk.

"I have tried these on every maiden in the village. Every maiden but one. I believe these belong to you, Redmaid," she said, holding up Red's abandoned shoes.

Red wasn't sure how to react. Her hand was still on the letter.

Cecilia looked closely at Red's face, searching again. She noticed the puffiness beneath Red's eyes, and the smeared remnants of eye makeup that Red hadn't bothered to wash off.

"Oh, Red. I'm sorry."

Red flinched.

"Yesterday, I made you do something I knew you didn't want to do. I shouldn't have been surprised that it went… unfavorably," Cecilia said slowly.

Red's eyes welled with tears.

"You're crying."

Cecilia gently wiped a tear from Red's eye. Her face and hand lingered closely for one electric pause before she leaned in for the kiss.

Red's eyes widened with shock before closing in pleasant surprise. The air around her crackled. Despite the cold drizzle, Red filled with warmth. She felt a shift within her chest cavity, as if dark clouds there finally blew away. She felt light.

Cecilia broke away, her face uncertain. Red's hand was still in her pocket. She took a deep breath and crumpled the letter into obsolescence.

"I'm sorry," Red said.

Cecilia embraced her.

It was the right thing to say.

Pamela Sneed

Pamela Sneed, author of *Imagine Being More Afraid of Freedom Than Slavery* (Henry Holt), *KONG,* and other works by Vintage Entity Press, is a New York-based poet, playwright, actress, voice-over performer, professor, and mentor. Her work is featured in *New York Times Magazine* (including the cover), *The New Yorker*, *BOMB* magazine, and *Time Out*, to name a few.

Interview

I.B. Why do you write?

P.S. I write because I have to. It's my way of making sense of the world, communicating, healing, seeing, breathing.

I.B. Describe how you discovered your voice as a writer?

P.S. In undergrad I had invited some women drummers I met through an internship in East Harlem to perform at my college. They agreed, but one of the women said I will only perform if you recite a poem. I agreed, and it was magic. I got a standing ovation.

I.B. Tell about a time when you felt like your work as an activist incited positive and evident social change.

P.S. I went to South Africa and performed for the women's organization FEW. It was standing room only. A lot of women were activists, a lot were involved with the dismantling of apartheid, some were a younger generation of women, and there were lesbian and trans folks, too. They expressed never having heard anything like my work, and I know I gave a lot of them voice.

I.B. What is one of the most challenging obstacles you've had to face in your writing life? How did you overcome it?

P.S. There are challenges I am still overcoming—writing in mixed form when people only want you to work in one, making political work and being acknowledged in the mainstream. The hardest obstacle I have overcome was when I had writers block after writing my first book, I*magine Being More Afraid of Freedom Than Slavery*. I realize now that I was in a transition, but the words wouldn't come out on paper. I have found that the way to handle a block is not to push it, but to accept it and let yourself rest. Meanwhile, trust that the words/story is growing inside of you and that it will come out when its safe.

I.B. It is common for people's definitions of success to revolve around financial and social status. Are these the terms you use to define success? If not, how do you define success?

P.S. I don't think you can enter a writer/performers life and think you will make tons of money. Some do; most don't. My personal success is measured by the work I've done/how many people I've freed, and helped come to voice.

I.B. What/who do you like to read?

P.S. I like a lot of the new African Literature by women, fiction, essays, social commentary, newspaper articles. I love science fiction, and Toni Morrison is my all-time favorite author.

I.B. What words of wisdom do you have for women who write?

P.S. Keep going, don't ever stop and in the words of Audre Lorde, make work as if yours or someone else's life depends upon it.

Donia Mounsef

Donia Mounsef was born and lived in Beirut, Lebanon until the age of 19. She is a Canadian poet, playwright and dramaturge. Her writing has been published and anthologized in *The Toronto Quarterly, The Labor of Love, Spitting Image, Bluestem, Yes Poetry, Gutter Eloquence, Poetry Quarterly, Below 40 Anthology.* Her performance poetry and plays have been performed on stages in Toronto, Montréal, Vancouver, Edmonton, and New Haven.

Interview

I.B. Why do you write?

D.M. I write because not writing is not an option: writing has always been a form of survival for me, a way to slow down, and stop for a moment, linger in the space of the in-between, take the time to savor, to catch and release words, sentiments, states, and thoughts that otherwise escape us in our frantic existence. What comes out (mostly in poetic form although I also write plays and fiction) has to take that shape because poetry allows me to enter in dialogue with myself and the other, in the many languages I inhabit, without judgment, without a need to justify the choices I make. With poetry, I can be in front of change and consistency at the time: it is like looking at the tide, it reminds us that we are permanent and impermanent at once. The poetic form is the only form that tells us if the word "bark" bites, if a wall is a mistake, if we can find our way home.

I.B. If you were a book, what book would you be? Why?

D.M. If I were a book I would be Adrienne Rich's poetry collection, *Fox,* because it was from this collection that I heard her read live for the first time. Her voice, her presence and her incredible way of connecting with the audience confirmed why she will always be my favorite poet, may she rest in peace.

I.B. Do you consider yourself a feminist? If so, how do YOU define feminism?

D.M. I consider myself a Feminist with capital F. I recently heard Stuart Hall say in an interview: "Feminism taught me the difference between a conviction in the head and a change in the way you live." May he also rest in peace. As bell hooks so aptly pointed out, "feminism is a passionate politics". Without it everyone is oppressed not just women, because the fight for gender equality is a fight for equality across the spectrum.

I.B. Share something interesting about yourself that has nothing to do with writing/ publishing.

D.M. I am an avid baller (basketball) and can sink the baseline shot with high accuracy, otherwise, I dominate the defensive boards (just sayin').

I.B. You have been given an opportunity to write the last sentence you will ever write. What is that sentence?

D.M. ... and peace came upon this land riding on a donkey.

Against Grammar

"What will we do with love? You said
While we were packing our suitcases
Do we take it with us, or hang it in the closet?
I said: let it go wherever it wants
It has already outgrown our collar and spread."
Mahmoud Darwish

Where you see walls I see openings
where you see windows I see shattered glass
snipers holes
hands reaching
skin stretched to "yes"
I want to give you everything
to "no", I have nothing to give you
to I don't know where we stand
to I know without a shadow of a doubt
where we lay
slow caresses, moans of a winter gale
on a lonesome naked harbor
hiding in the pine trees
leaning like divers about to leap to the sea
under a frozen night sky

where are we?
what are we to each other?
the edge of my shore, you are my Pender Harbour
a drop of water in my heart saltier than tears
collects furtively in the corner of your eye
mapping your quiet sorrow
to a hand you use to speak

a language dancing on stage boards made of silence
to a guttural language I speak and you like to relish
leaving my throat one syllable after another
at the speed of trains departing a war zone

after so many years
so many moons of linguistic exile
do you know how it is
not to feel in your mother tongue?
and my mother tongue is a heavy suitcase
I inherited from the hands of an aging father
who packed it for me carefully
before he bid me goodbye that night
at the port of Jounieh
a suitcase made of sounds
single utterances
murmurs in my head
glances of his eyes and I am his eyes
between rounds of bullets and scattered children
islands in the frozen sea we call family

do you know how it is
to dream in a foreign language?
we do speak a different language
love is a verb we conjugate with the body
in different word order
subject verb object ify me
how do you explain
why my hand speaks so well the language
of the small of your back?
how did you learn so quickly
the geography of pebbles in the palm of my hand?

there is no certainty in language
for the likes of us
who love with the tenacity of flood tides

who give with the generosity of the sea
in total disregard for the rules of navigation

what is the tide?
but mutiny against the shore
what is love?
but sedition against grammar

Arils

the small bowl filled with pomegranate arils
teeters at the edge of sleep and want
your body taught me the meaning of that word
when your mischief placed them
in the hollow of your neck
between your breasts, at the cavernous sternum
in the belly button
I savor the uncertainty
guiding them and letting them roll off
your hot and cold skin
like glassy pebbles in the uprush
they stop at times by themselves
leaning their white tips
to listen to your heartbeat
your unruly body weaving dreams
with light and red liquid
counting star-shaped points
on flesh overcast with slumber
squeezing the bloody juice with my teeth
awakens your need
an ever so subtle jolt of cold liquor
I lick ever so lightly, frivolously
my reddened tongue lingers
between your lemony folds
to translate your foreign language
into the Braille relief flexed muscles form
molded for knowing when to open up
and when to shelter from thundery desire

Desire Path

"A desire path is a path created by usage, not a predetermined path. Normally these paths are created by people taking shortcuts across fields to get from Point A to Point B more quickly than the pre-determined paths (like sidewalks) that have been put in place."
Gaston Bachelard, The Poetics of Space

I carried you as a burden
an amulet
a case of beer
a compass for a new frontier
a brave light
for the dark west
sitting under a bridge
near a sleepy coastline
I showed you the place I came from
roads I travelled
between south and north
Sioufi and Sassine
maps drawn on an awkward body
the arrow in my chest at thirteen
the girl trapped inside the boy
the ductile dream inside the harsh decoy

if one day you come looking for me
under the carob tree
follow the desire path
worn out casually by young footprints
touch the earth beneath our fear
the shortest distance between two women
countless steps that come from nowhere

and go nowhere
you will find me
a shadow without a body
a pale contour on washed out earth
fading into the moonlight
between two shooting stars

Chris Shorne

Chris Shorne's work appears in *Make/Shift Magazine*, *Sinister Wisdom*, and *Saltwater Quarterly,* as well as on the stage with TumbleMe Production's "Forever or Whatever: A Homoromantic Confession." She is an MFA candidate at Antioch University Los Angeles.

Interview

I.B. Why do you write?

C.S. I write because I have yet to find a reason not to.

I.B. If you were a book, what book would you be? Why?

C.S. If I had to be a book—which I hope never happens because I really prefer being a human—I would be something like *Being Peace* by Thich Nhat Hanh. What better way to practice being.

I.B. Do you consider yourself a feminist? If so, how do YOU define feminism?

C.S. Yes, I consider myself a feminist. I remember the first time I saw that bumper sticker: "Feminism is the radical notion that women are people." And I thought, and still think, that pretty well sums it up.

I.B. Share something interesting about yourself that has nothing to do with writing/publishing.

C.S. I can crack my ears. (You know, like you would crack your knuckles).

I.B. You have been given an opportunity to write the last sentence you will ever write. What is that sentence?

C.S. *Who knows?*

Exchanging Goods and Services to Meet Needs; or, Economy

After Chrystos

"Scarcity and self-interest are the primary forces of modern economics."
—any economics textbook

It's true. I drink a glass of water—empty the cup—now you can't drink it.

And if you stand next to me, if we both look out the window and drink in
the view of Mt. Rainier, is each view now worth less?

Scarcity: What is swallowed.

In anthropology I was taught about an economic system where the people give their goods to one person in their community. And that person redistributes those goods. The people choose for this position the one who is—of all the people—known to be the most generous.

I know I'm not
a generous poet, but…my lover—

god, no matter how much of her
breast I suck into my mouth, she has

more. No matter how often she brushes
my cheeks with those breasts, one on either side,

she does not become less
soft. I bring as much of her—ample & butch—into as much

of me as I can, over and over and always

she is still full.

Not everything that goes in a mouth is a commodity.

Often she is over-full, which is a nice way of saying horny
and horny is a way
of saying sometimes the need to share is so strong it's uncomfortable.

Generosity can be selfish.

My words I keep. Stuffed away as if they will feed me in my lean times. I suck small stones into my mouth, lift shoulders up, cinch my jaw like a satchel and let the rocks pile and dry until I am so full of holding that I almost believe that chalky taste that grates against my teeth is satiety.

But the bright lover comes to me, fat
and wanting. She wants my mouth open, again
she is pulling scarce stories from under my lips, unlocking
my jaw, loosing the words. I feel them

drop off. They clack together;
pool on the couch where she sits. She slides her hand
across them—all of them—leans back
to smile, and says, "Delicious."

My mouth, released, at last,
smiles back: Yes
those modern-day economists are right. This economy is
a gift, after all it is

out of her own self-interest that she gives me
my own
empty.

Essential Elements of Spring

1. unopened book
2. green underwear
3. openhinged

1.
take the book out of your backpack. bring it to your bedside table. turn on the reading lamp. get in bed. have a sip of water. look out the window at dark sky and dark trees. get up. open the window. sniff like a dog. get back in bed. watch cloud pull away from cloud. watch your lover take off her shirt. good. take off yours. press spongy body against spongy body. absorb; be absorbed.

2.
mix the sound of the alarm with the birds in your dream with the crows on the phone line outside your window. you have opened your eyes. turn. back to the sky, see unopened books blurry foreground, lovers breasted background. clearly now, she takes off her pants. briefs: green. pull. her and the sky blue back in. crows call in her pupils; call you: unopened spring. so prop your lids up. watch calendula open orange. swallow. swallow again.

3.
where she licks your toes while you're dreaming. where one toe, then a whole foot goes into swamp. swamp fed from the mouth. the mouth that streamed, streamed from the heat at the bottom of glacier. glacier that formed between tops of mountains. those mountains that once cradled glacier as snow. wake to place; yourself under her. now. river if you must. become light, green that grows from the source of a Spring, hinging—
on a thousand-year-old winter.

Heather Warren

Heather Warren is a poet and musician from Fairbanks, Alaska. She is currently working on an MFA in poetry at the University of Alaska Fairbanks and loves the below-zero temperatures of winter. She lives in a dry cabin with her dog Diggory.

Interview

I.B. Why do you write?

H.W. I see writing as a way to further understand myself. It's a continual process of emotional experience and observation. Through writing and other creative outlets, I feel as if I can speak to myself and I can speak to others. Writing is the best way to give myself a voice and I hope it inspires others to do so as well.

I.B. If you were a book, what book would you be? Why?

H.W. Reading Jeanette Winterson's novel *Written on the Body* made me feel like I *can't* write but that I *can* write, at the same time. I read the first page over and over for three days! If I were a book, this would be it, as it represents to me one of the most important realizations I've embraced: love, relationships, and life are all contextual and full of uncertainties.

I.B. Do you consider yourself a feminist? If so, how do YOU define feminism?

H.W. Yes. Absolutely. I consider myself a feminist. It's surprising to me that such a large amount of people reject the term. And when I enter these discussions, I ask, well do you think women should have rights? Do you agree that we should all exist within a safe space? Have you noticed that almost every woman you talk to has some type of story to share, of an experience in which she felt uncomfortable, unsafe, violated? So if you agree with those questions, what's the problem in embracing feminism? Why, because the term is loaded? Well, what word isn't. I define feminism as the fight for a safe space. And with domestic violence and sexual assault rates remaining ridiculously high in this country, especially within my state, I feel like feminism is needed more than ever.

I.B. Share something interesting about yourself that has nothing to do with writing/publishing?

H.W. I beatbox and play percussion for a band called Zingaro Roots. Latin/gypsy/folk in Fairbanks, Alaska!

I.B. You have been given an opportunity to write the last sentence you will ever write. What is that sentence?

H.W. The clicking clacking of the rope smacking the pavement is my rising pulse.

Monkey Bars

There is a young girl hanging. The space behind her knees grips a monkey bar tight. The boys who live nearby chant: climb it.

Wisps of hair sweep the gravel and the girl laughs at this game. The boys laugh at this game and the game is only encouraging more laughs but this laughter is only a fleeting representation of this moment, "Let's see how long she can hang there with her knees!"

The boys are bored and the girl is hanging.

The blood rushes to her head and oh Goddess! who knows what else.

River Babies

Troubled Mothers / Darkness does not leave this place / There are babies drowning in rivers with only few swimmers / with only few arms to wrap around few babies / there are babies that will drown.

It is, a hot hot thing.

There are babies that will drown with only few swimmers / the river is an overflow of lost children with no mothers and no fathers and if these children have mothers and fathers / then they are abandoned / to fend for themselves.

There are fathers who beat mothers and those mothers beat themselves / and each father who thinks he owns a beaten mother is / a baby in the river / and each mother who cannot leave a beater father whether she wants to or doesn't want to is / a baby in the river.

There is a current in the mind that the swimmer must follow / There is a current in the body that the swimmer must follow / There is a current in sex that the swimmer must follow before the swimmer can swim and help a baby / rescue their own selves.

There is only so far that a swimmer can swim before the swimmer drowns with a baby.

My Mother Dreams About My Lover and I Hiding in A Cave

where we wait with the indefinite
and cuddle bats, without a knapsack
or a match, and our toes
are pinched immobile by fallen rocks.

Maybe it was the boy you picked?
            It's not about picking boys.

Have you tried another boy?
            I try them on like outfits

discarded to the floor, I watch her.
My lover, loves to take off my
underwire, straps
a compression vest
around my chest then says,
you look handsome.

I spread my legs she says my legs are spread I bend over she says I bend over she says get between my legs I am between her legs lifting each leg onto each shoulder, though I am not enough.

Changming Yuan

Changming Yuan, six-time Pushcart nominee and author of *Chansons of a Chinaman* (2009) and *Landscaping* (2013), grew up in rural China but currently tutors in Vancouver, where he co-publishes *Poetry Pacific* with Allen Qing Yuan and operates *PP Press*. With a Ph.D. in English, Yuan has recently been interviewed by *[PANK]*, and has poetry appearing in *Best Canadian Poetry, BestNewPoemsOnline, Exquisite Corpse, London Magazine, Threepenny Review,* and 769 other literary journals/anthologies across 28 countries.

Interview

I.B. Why do you write?

C.Y. I write because there is too much in my heart or on my mind.

I.B. If you were a book, what book would you be? Why?

C.Y. If I were a book, I wish to be *Dao De Jing*, because it is full of human wisdom and natural poetry.

I.B. Do you consider yourself a feminist? If so, how do YOU define feminism?

C.Y. Yes, I consider myself a feminist. To me, feminism means the full recognition of and true respect for all women's rights.

I.B. Share something interesting about yourself that has nothing to do with writing/ publishing?

C.Y. I am a landlord/property manager who has just gotten rid of an evil tenant in Vancouver, more or less as in the 1990 Hollywood movie *Pacific Heights*.

I.B. You have been given an opportunity to write the last sentence you will ever write. What is that sentence?

C.Y. "What else can I say to this snakeland?"

Poetry Pacific

29 Sept 2014

November

Most monotonous month:
Each passing day is depressed
Into a crow, its wings
Its body and tails
Newly glazed in the mists
Of thick dusk
Though its heart still
Lingers in the memory of
Summer's orange morning glows

Mango

Textured with
Presented in the shape of
All female tenderness

As smooth as sleek
As fantasy, where, and whereby
Let

Man go

No, nobody knows this
But you are really no more
Or no less than the old
Egyptian metonymy of
A stream, river, lake, sea or
Even an entire ocean, where
There is always water, where
There are always fish
Rather than a synecdochic Z
Pushed straight upright
On the bank of the Euphrates

To Mars: A Free Sonnet

How do we love thee? Let us count the ways:
We love thee to the very limits of high-science
The boundaries of technologies, the frontiers of
The human conscience; in particular we love thy
Art of work on a mother feeding her baby in a
Shelter, a sheep boy driving his little herd to the
Valley, or a crowd of country lads celebrating a
Wedding. More important, we love the way thou
Help us to get rid of all extra food processors
In the human shape: the poor, the sick, the weak
The old, all wanted or unwanted others, above all
We love the way thou have become a real game as
Bloodily vivid as a movie on a vast colored screen
Thousands of miles far, far away in another world

Should You Allow

Should you allow us to live, let it not like robots
Running and working around the clock, to give you
All the comfort and convenience available to human
Masters. Should you allow us to live, o let us live
With the kind of freedom you enjoy, the equal rights
And democracy you are talking about so aloud
So that our tears and sweat will become less salty
Than our blood, our eyes less murky than our visions
Then even the food and products we make would warm
Your hearts. Don't try to make love with us only to fulfil
Your sense of conquest, or beat us mad, containing us
Whistling your dogs of war upon us when you have
A nightmare. True, like robots we may not be entitled
To your human rights, but even a cornered robot rabbit will bite back
Someday, somehow, like a treaded cobra, like your fore fathers

Sasha Tamar Strelitz

Sasha Tamar Strelitz is a long-time poet and literary analyst. In her 27 years, she has lived in South Florida, New York City, Tel Aviv, Israel, and now Orlando, Florida. She is currently working towards a Master's in literature at the University of Central Florida. A doctoral program is in her imminent future.

Interview

I.B. Why do you write?

S.S. Writing is instinctual for me. Like a pang of hunger or a yawn that signals, "time for sleep" or a sexual impulse, I feel a deep-rooted urge to write. It's an irrationality stemming from my lizard brain.

I.B. If you were a book, what book would you be? Why?

S.S. If I had to be a book, I'd be an anthology that would include: Ancient Greek writings on the muses, Indian mythology, Arthurian poetry, Medieval-Renaissance Kabbalist writings, imagination-based Romantic poetry + poetic statements + short stories, Transcendentalist essays and poetry (including Whitman and Dickinson), and Beat Generation works.

I.B. Do you consider yourself a feminist? If so, how do YOU define feminism?

S.S. I'm most definitely feminist. For me, feminism is *not* hairy pits and lesbian experimentation and forced football fandom (although it may be for some). Feminism runs deeper, as it seeks to muddy the stereotypical waters. Just because I'm without a phallus does not mean I'm incapable of intellectual and social proficiency. Just because a man is without certain anatomical procreative elements does not mean he's not sensitive and cannot cook brilliantly. As Virginia Woolf once said, "It is fatal to be a man or a woman pure and simple; one must be woman-manly or man-womanly." It's all about social equality so that generations to come won't fathom the Cult of Domesticity, so that everyone (mostly) agrees with Adrienne Rich.

I.B. Share something interesting about yourself that has nothing to do with writing/publishing?

S.S. I'm kind of a music nerd. I really dig the blues, jazz, reggae, "world," classic rock, and some downtempo acid jazz. In one day, I'll go from listening to Ravi Shankar's sitar strumming; to Billie Holiday's and Janis Joplin's sweet, painful moans; to Bob Marley's and Bob Dylan's jubilant, anti-inequality ditties; to hair-raising guitar solos by the Jimmies—Page and Hendrix; and then maybe some Air and Bonobo to shut it all down.

I.B. You have been given an opportunity to write the last sentence you will ever write. What is that sentence?

S.S. If I could write a last sentence, it'd have to be, "And then," Just like that. But, I'd also want to try and fit in the words "pain" and "beauty" somewhere.

A Meditation on the End

~Inspired by Allen Ginsberg, and dedicated to la familia Farji y mi Mami.

walk on down the hall…

like a frog on a lily pad, sitting contemplatively
(“dreaming back thru life, Your time—and mine accelerating”)
oh, cruel and causeless life
(*yitgal v’yidka*—
they were not ready)
the birds’ chirpchirpchirp > the mechanical whirring of the pool-pump motor

rooftops like that at 34th st. stir up sweet memories
(when they were here)
did they hear Black running after them?
(quickly catching up as always)
the constant *whirwhirwhir* soothes me, but the orange/yellow sounds of the sun’s rays
interrupt these thoughts
and also, the sun’s yellow/orange rays exhilarate me
(faintly whispered, “you breath in the Nile”)

¡rumination energizes and intensifies everything again!

bend + sit = easy
(ultimately, he^1 couldn’t bear it
and he^2 was spritely…but then he jumped)
he^1 catapulted me into the air ::splash::
(playing *The Little Mermaid*)
in my heart, i know that one day—*chus v’chalila, pe pe pe*—we’ll all be with he^1 and he^2

shema Israel, Adonai Elohainu, Adonai echad
(“strange now to think of you, gone”)

it plays with my hair and dries the tears off my cheeks
    ("work of the Merciful Lord of Poetry")
the awesome Blue soars — expansive, boundless
    (there they are)

to their female soulmates, a meditation on the End
    (chirp chirpchirp chirp chirpchirp chirp (it's them))

Summertime and the Living

"Ani rotzah t'marim, ach'shav" (*reish* pronounced like the *erre*); her laughter like clucking bouncing off the hashish haze, ricocheting off the tapestry-covered walls
Thinking about the pyramids of dates on that truck that gave her a lift 3 hours ago, she drooled slightly; thirst abated by a Parliament Light
The Galgalatz DJ announced MJ—in a whirl, she got up, cig in mouth, body sticky from stagnant sweat; steaming swivels of incense interrupted by her movement
Wanna be startin' somethin'—
Everything rhythmically swayed with her; the room seemed to dance with the bomb shelter under it
Crinkle. Rip. Crush. Grind. Place. Roll. Smoke, and
exchanging cig for jay, one more toke—GHB flashback—glimmer subsided, eyes dulled, depression juices surged, and all because of that almost-faded hickey
Empty, devoid of trustworthiness, LOST , she watched Tabula Rasa for the third time: "Iteration #..."—she thought ahead to the Walkabout, to the White Rabbit, to Humpty Dumpty
Then, no beamish boy, she chortled and burbled: "it's brillig and twenty, time to gyre a j"[1]
Crinkle. Rip. Crush. Grind. Place. Roll. Smoke, and
"One two! One two! And through and through,"[2] pregger-pause, "what's vorpal? Hmmm . . ."

---

[1] Carroll, Lewis. *The Looking-Glass and What Alice Found There*. New York: Rand, McNally, & Co., 1917. Web. 2 July 2013.

[2] Ibid.

She Insisted, "Gematria!"

She
is an artist,
          dreamer,
                    stargazer,
Bohemian&rebel
with rings on her fingers
and bells on her shoes
(and she was into the blues)
                              Live in the now!
                                                  (aka New-Agey bullshit)
Tattoos are for goyim,
patchouli is for
hippie-dipsters
Virginia is for   loverrrs.
          She (or her)
          incessantly burns incense
          and also she
          diffuses oils for
          the wicked insomnia
          (18,000 attempts at meditation).
The big O moment
spray-painted in
pink and purple dressed
in
black*
                                                            *(sincere attempt to incorporate
                                                              more color)
                              Soft skin
                              cute smile
                              (like Botwin and Silverman)
                              Look at those mascaraed

eyes fluttering
to the beat beat beat
of their own drum
(drum drum…
OCD)
P.S. 200 40 400 5 300 60
!!!!!!!5 40 6 60 100 1 10 5

Made in the USA
Charleston, SC
19 April 2014